# THE WARLORD'S CONCUBINE

J.E. & M. KEEP

ISBN-13: 978-1-988619-11-8

# DEDICATION

To our friends who didn't judge, readers of The Keep back when we were first starting out, and Darknest Fantasy Erotica who encouraged us to keep going.

# CONTENTS

# ACKNOWLEDGMENTS

J.E. & M. Keep recognize that erotica can be very personal, and that everyone has their limits on what they wish to read. Because of this, we provide content warnings for all our erotica so that you can avoid any **triggering material** – or find the story you most want to read. If you want your book spoiler free, please skip this section!
This particular story contains cock worship, size differences, concubines, breeding, reluctance, dubious consent, oral sex, all set in a dark fantasy world.

# CHAPTER 1

Never had the two women seen the city so lit up at night. Not even during the harvest festival when the alchemists set off their fireworks would the great spires and steeples of Ariste City be so illuminated in the pitch black of night.

The city of Ariste was like a semi-circle at the base of a mountain. The grace and majesty of the capital was unsurpassed, even in the southern empire that stretched so far and wide. The buildings were made from great white stones harvested from the northern desert, marble from the Quelan Empire and rich wood from the forests of the Ariste mountains southern slopes. Each tall spire was a stunning monument to decadence and ingenuity.

The natural topography made it a rich and moist land on the other side, but there in the city itself it tended to be dry and temperate. That fact, the princess feared, would mean the fires that consumed her glorious city-state below would not be quenched any time soon.

Worse still, the tall elegant princess Anabelle Flair thought as she clutched her handmaiden's hands, were the sounds of destruction coming from her mighty palace below. When news of the city walls breach reached her, she was already at the height of the palace, which sat up the slope of Ariste Mountain, overlooking the city. It was so easy to ignore the rabble from the cold, northern steppes on her high perch, but now they were not only in her city, she could hear them in her home.

The crash of priceless pottery and the smashing of antique wood doors, carved from ancient timber continued, and it made the pale, slender Anabelle shake. "Mirella," the gold-haired princess' voice trembled, "where will we go?"

The answer was obvious. Nowhere. High atop that central tower of the palace, there were only two options. Surrender to the hairy savages of the northern steppes, whom the state of Ariste had kept at bay for millennium with its great walls and cunning.

Or she could throw herself from the great glass windows to crash lifelessly upon the burning city below.

How could the handmaiden get that through the mind of the pampered princess staring at her with wide, saucer-like blue eyes?

Mirella's hands went to her princess' jaw,

holding her and staring at her with those intense, green eyes. The handmaiden's skin was darker than most people of Ariste, an exotic olive tone. Her glossy, black hair was pinned back off of her face in a careful, almost regal manner, though her clothes easily classified her status within the walls.

Still, with that calm ease that had endeared her to the royal family, her voice was stern, "I will stay with you. We will speak with them—reason with them. They won't hurt you, my loving princess, provided you obey. Do what they ask of you and you'll live to fight again. Do not struggle or fuss, and I will stay at your side. I promise, I'll find a way for you to get out of this."

It was all so even handed, with not a lick of fear tingeing her voice. Even though Ariste was secluded, Mirella had dealt with many different people from many different walks of life in her youth. She knew that the best thing to do was to succumb, to get through the moment and plan for the next day's success. She had seen over thirty five hard years, of toil and hard work, and though her flesh was still smooth, she was wiser than the young woman before her.

The frail little princess steadied her nerves at those reassuring words and nodded. Dressed in only her nightgown, it was still an extravagant garment, white and gossamer, studded with pearls as it clung to her slender waist before ballooning out in courtly fashion.

"We shall per—" The words couldn't leave her delicate little peach lips fast enough before the door at the end of the hall burst open. The lock had been set by Mirella, but the wood was now splintered and destroyed. A chunk of the formerly elegant door knocked over a corner table and sent a priceless vase from the far south to shatter on the floor.

With a great shriek the princess once again pulled away, still holding Mirella's hands and trying to put the handmaid between the barbarians and herself.

The barbarians of the northern steppes were never seen in the courts of Ariste. Though they had traded continually with the city state over the millennia, they were considered savages, and rarely allowed even within the city walls.

The two that pushed through were typical of their kind. Tall and broad, they were a mix of pale white and a wind-blasted ruddy hue. The steppes were cold and cloudy in the north, and they saw little sun despite their crude dress of furs and leather. They were renowned for their hairiness. Their barrel chests, arms, legs and faces were covered in it, and those two with their clubs were prime examples.

Mirella stood in front of the princess. At their entrance, she let go of the woman's hand and dropped to her knees. Her face tilted down demurely, but her voice rang through loud and far prouder than a handmaiden's voice should be. "Sirs, we request to see your leader. He will not wish for the princess to be harmed."

Her voice managed to carry above the sounds of destruction from out of the now open door, but it didn't quell the two savages as they advanced on the two women.

Anabelle shrieked again, curling up in the corner against the window and white stone wall and covered herself. They grabbed both women by their hair, and the stench of their sweaty musk was pungent as they were dragged across the marble flooring several feet.

"Quiet, Princess! Please!" Mirella begged the woman, even as her face contorted in pain as her feet scrambled to keep her aloft and relieve the tension on her scalp. "It will be all right!"

The only thing to bring the sight to a halt was the sound of a booming voice that seemed to emanate from beyond their world. "He does not wish it indeed," came the commanding tone, and as quickly as the two brutes had resorted to savagery they released the women's hair and collapsed to their knees in obeisance and fear.

Mirella grunted as she fell, but instantly she moved to her ward, her slender arm slipping around the Princess' shoulders. Her dressing gown was far drabber and less elaborate, but it was still of fine quality and kept her wholly covered, for which she was at least modestly grateful for as she stared towards the strange voice. She kneeled, and guided the princess to do the same, following suite of their two, cruel captors.

The princess was stubborn however. A life of ruling made her resist bowing before anyone even then, and so she was sat up as the source of that husky voice came through the door.

As if from out of the shadow, the tall, dark figure strode silently down the marble lined hall. The light from the inflamed city below was the only thing giving sight to the man, for unlike the other savages, he was dark in every manner.

Easily bigger and taller than either of the two brutes that had busted down the door, the monumental charcoal-coloured man looked nothing like the other savages aside from his size.

Where they were pale, he was a pure and unearthly dark. Where they were hairy, he was smooth. Where they wore ragged armour, he wore little more than a fine uneven cloak that draped from one shoulder down across to another hip, leaving half of his torso exposed and nude. His garb, especially those high boots of his, were strange and exotic. They were not the crude assemblage of animal hide like the other savages, but they were neither of Ariste nor the southern Empire that Mirella could tell.

The two women could feel the odd man's intense gaze upon them even as his eyes were hidden by the shadows. The brutes that were hauling them away but moments before dared not move or utter a thing. The brazen princess—too privileged to know when to shut her mouth—spoke up in a haughty, quavering voice, "I am the rightful heir to the Kingdom of Ariste, and you are tres—"

Reaching out in a flash of speed that belied his large size, he wrapped his black gloved fingers about the Princess's slender stalk of a neck, choking all words and air from her. So close, the two women could see the smooth, outline of his muscular flesh, the bulge of pecs, abs and below that of his startlingly large groin beneath black leather.

Mirella gasped at the strange sight before her. Her hair was mussed up from her rough handling, but she didn't care much at the sight of what was surely a god. Her lips dropped open and it quickly made sense to her why they would attack, and she couldn't help that a gasp of awe and benevolence passed her lips, or the fact that her eyes wouldn't stop working over his body again and again.

The charcoal coloured giant had obsidian hair like the savages, but instead of being frazzled and wiry like theirs, it was sleek and glossy like Mirella's. It flowed long down over his shoulders like a lion's mane, framing his broad, ethereally handsome face, though some of it was put together in the back in a silver ring.

Releasing the Princess's throat at last, leaving the reddened woman to cough and sputter for breath on her hands and knees, he methodically brought his gaze from the blonde royalty to the handmaiden. When he spoke once more it was with an eerily gravely tone, so full of masculinity and virility, but seeming totally inhuman. "The princess is to be my newest concubine," he stated firmly, though his eyes were locked on Mirella's, as if boring through her to her soul.

Her breathing caught, which was something quite unexpected for the in-control handmaiden. Her lips quirked just a tiny bit as her head bowed, but she couldn't draw her eyes away from his, no matter how much she wanted to. "Your will is not to be debated," she finally managed out, and the breathy manner that she said it was filled with awe.

Loose tendrils of hair lay against her face, the heavy strands returning to their normal position with a brief primping, and Mirella couldn't help but do so. The last thing she wanted was this god to see her looking less than her best. "I am certain my envy knows no bounds."

The savages beside her twitched, and the handmaiden got the impression that she had committed some taboo merely by speaking directly to the giant. Neither budged to reprimand her, as if held in place by something stronger still than reverence for their lord; fear.

It was hard for Mirella to tell in the dark, but she could swear she made out a half-smile in the shadows of his face. The princess coughed through her choking, and gasped in air, "Concubine?! I'll never—" and she received a backhanding. Mirella knew it intimately. It wasn't intended to hurt the princess, it was intended to humiliate and quiet her. It was the act of a master to his slave, and it did its job, for the princess—so unaccustomed to anything but absolute submission—squealed and toppled to the marble floor from the strike.

Without word the dark man turned, and the two savages scrambled away as if their lives depended on it—and perhaps did—leaving the chamber. The dark prince announced in his booming voice, "Hold the two of them for my concubines to claim."

Her own lips curled but she wiped away the grin, instead tending to her Princess, though the motions had somehow shifted. She remained dutiful, but something lurked behind her eyes that the

Princess would never know to suspect in her older handmaiden.

# CHAPTER 2

They saw no more men that night, and it wasn't until the red of dawn broke on the horizon that the two women were visited again. Startled from their uneasy rest, it wasn't more of the savage men that came for them, but two women.

Obviously of the same northern stock, they were tall, strong, with black hair either tied back in a ponytail or cut no longer than their jaws. They had harsh looks on their faces, and though Mirella could tell they had a certain attraction to them, their ragged furs and harsh demeanours did not make her think of concubines.

With hands on the large, curved knives at their waists, they watched the two of them in creepy silence. It was only the princess, of course, to break the quiet, "What are they doing here, Mirella?" she demanded in what was supposed to be a whisper, but hardly sufficed as one. "I won't be that dark spawn's concubine! You said everything would be alright, you said—" she struggled with her own overwhelming outrage and worry.

"Everything will be all right," she said, though her eyes remained locked on the two women. "Sometimes you have to do things you don't want to in order to see another morning, my loving Princess. This is one of those times. I realize this must be difficult for you, but if you keep a cool head, you will make things easier on yourself."

She had only slept restlessly, yet her face barely registered the lack of sleep. She had become so used to just scraping by with what she could get that she seemed almost fresh, especially compared to the red faced princess.

"Where's father?" the princess insisted, "He went out with the army to find out what happened to the Forward Guard! He should have been back by now!" she exclaimed, stress in her haughty but frail voice. Of course, the possibility that the reason why they were now prisoners might have been due to the King's death with his troops was not entertained in her mind.

"Princess, just focus on remaining alive. When your father returns for you, he will care for and avenge you, but you must live to see that day," she lied so easily, so calmly, that it was hard to pick up on. Mirella was a practical, mid-age woman and understood what had happened quite clearly—a god had overtaken the town, and now they were to serve.

She had served all her life, and for her, this was a promotion. For the Princess...

Mirella's face turned to her blonde ward and the soft smile that touched her eyes was sympathetic, "You just simply must behave while you are here. Do as you are asked, and you will see your father soon."

The pale little princess looked almost dumbfounded by her handmaiden's suggestion. With a weak shove of her frail little arms to the other woman she scoffed haughtily, "Mirella, I am no serving woman. When father returns he shall not find me... de-... de—" she flustered, her pale features going such a deep hue of red, she simply couldn't' say 'defiled'.

"If you have a way that you can keep your purity and your head, Princess, I would love to know it. I can simply assure you that the god will not smile kindly on disobedience. I know this is a bitter concoction, but I only want what is best for you," her green eyes stared into the ice blue of her employer, bidding her acquiescence.

Staring at her in utter disbelief and horror, Princess Annabelle visibly recoiled. "God?" she said with such complete distaste.

Before she had a chance to blaspheme any further, the two female guards thudded their chests with their fists and bowed their heads. "The God-King has chosen you both," they said in their savage voices, so much harsher than the ladies of court. "You will come now and be taken to his tent, where no man shall touch or look upon you until you have been made his," they declared with the certainty of fanatics.

Suddenly the actions of the men the night before made sense; they couldn't reprimand chosen concubines of their God-King. They couldn't even look at them, let alone hurt or speak to them.

Mirella felt a smug sense of satisfaction at having so quickly and accurately understood his status, but she looked nothing more than sympathetic. "See, Princess? He will protect you. You just have to be good. He will be able to return you to your father in good faith." Her lies would soon unravel, she realized, but it didn't matter.

She and the princess were on equal footing now. The princess was just too daft to realize it.

True to their words, the female guards escorted them out through the palace and nary a male dared look upon them. The two guards themselves were immune to this, having to speak with and yell at the occasional savage, but none dared look at Mirella or Anabelle as they were escorted through the ruins of the once decadent palace.

For her part, the dainty princess gasped and looked shocked at all the signs of carnage. Every door was seemingly broken open, most of the pottery smashed, and rare was it to see a painting that was still intact, never were they still hung on the wall. The accumulated culture and riches of a royal line that extended back nearly five thousand years was utterly in ruin after only a single night. The frail woman looked about ready to faint from it all, though was thankfully made speechless.

Somehow it was the sight of the expertly crafted

wooden doors in a heap at the main entry hall—piled high for fires for the camped out barbarians—that got to the princess the most and she screamed in fruitless anger. "Savages!"

Mirella was at best annoyed by the wanton carnage. For years she had coveted the wealth of the castle and to see it ruined was both satisfactory and disappointing. If she couldn't have it, she was pleased that no one could, yet it did little to help her personally. Her hand rested on the shoulder of the princess, but she barely cared to console the woman as instead she stared at the men disallowed from looking at her, musing to herself thoughtfully.

Apparently the God-King did not reside within the conquered palace, for the mighty tent—made of some thick, stretched hide it seemed—dominated the courtyard outside the palace proper, still overlooking the smoking ruins of Ariste below.

It sloped along in a strange pattern that made the tent itself look spiked and ominous, and all about the outside of it were arrayed pikes, holding the heads of slain men. Most soldiers, though there were the occasional nobles, and Anabelle finally fainted when she saw the visage of a man she once knew from court.

Mirella caught the woman, keeping her from hitting the marble walkway and injuring herself, but with an irritated look, the two guards kept them going ahead and into the tent.

Inside, the handmaiden found herself gazing upon something truly astounding.

It wasn't the decadence and wealth of the palace,

but it was something remarkable nonetheless. All about were strewn rich silk cushions, piled high in great mounds, upon which lounged other women in various states of undress or duress. Few had the appearance of the two guard women, but they stood watch. Most appeared to be other captives recently taken for the God-King following this conquest, and looked as confused and lost as did the haughty princess.

A great table filled the center of the tent, and upon it was heaped food. A mix of the rich pantry of the palace with the flavours of the harsh tundra, making for the oddest banquet Mirella had ever seen.

But at the heart of it stood a statue, carved from obsidian stone. It was unmistakable though the craftsmanship was not as refined as that of the courtly artists who decorated the millennia old palace. The presence of the mighty man, albeit nude and holding a great scimitar that was lodged into the spine of some defeated foe, inspired all the other women, even the guards, to fear. Mirella could tell they—unlike her—knew much greater terror of the God-King, even in his lifeless representation.

It was curious to her why the man of such taste would be so destructive, but it didn't matter. She barely glanced to the other women. The evening prior she might have been a handmaiden, but now she was on equal footing with all of them, and it filled her with a strange sense of righteousness. Her eyes worked over the statue as she left the princess to recover on top of some pillows, her gaze one of wonderment and a lingering, heated desire.

His power radiated from the stone and she briefly wondered at what the more skilled artisans could do for him.

She couldn't recall at how long she might've been staring at that statue when she was disturbed, her gaze lost on that harsh stone depiction, entranced by the generous proportions of his muscles and loins. It was, as far as she could tell, true to form, but lacking in the expert subtleties a court artisan would bring to it.

"Most don't even dare to look at it," came that otherworldly voice, so richly masculine, irradiating such strength and command in a manner she'd never heard before.

In the torchlight of the tent she could make him out all the clearer. His charcoal skin was smooth and flawless. His face so chiselled and handsome. Hair long and perfectly shiny. Her first guess only seemed all the more right; a god. Though with the dark clothes he wore, looking a blend of velvet and leather, mixed with his piercing dark gaze and skin, it didn't take much guessing to place as what kind of deity he might be.

She bowed before him so gracefully, filled with respect and awe, though her eyes didn't drop demurely as she felt that, perhaps, they should. Instead she was simply entranced with the man, and was an absolute slave to the need to see him fully, "They don't know what they're missing." She waited a heartbeat before adding, "What should I call you?"

She had taken some time on the walk over, prior to the Princess fainting, to fix her hair by some of the shattered mirrors. Though she certainly didn't look all she could—if only she had been able to steal some makeup from the Princess' room!—but she was quite the exotic beauty nonetheless. With her feminine curves under the soft material of her dressing gown, she looked quite lovely, especially knelt before him with such subservience.

The entirety of the sprawling tent was silent around her. She hadn't noticed the eerie silence descend as she stared at the statue, but now it was unmistakable. The other women were cowering away, shaking and looking petrified. None dared look in his direction though; not even the guards who seemed exceptionally trusted showed him the kind of obeisance Mirella did. In fact, they showed the same signs of fear, their eyes downcast, their positions shuffled away to the edges of the tent.

With a hand upon his hip, he strummed those strong fingers of his upon his waist and circled partly about her, standing near her side as he looked up over his own statue. In a rather conversational tone, the dark, otherworldly man spoke in his husky voice, "At least it keeps them from noticing the crude imitation of me this makes for."

Sliding his dark gaze down to her again, his broad chest pushed out and mostly visible with the half-cloak hardly covering him, he said, "'My Lord' is the most common term."

"I was just thinking the same thing and was wondering to myself if any artisan still lives, My Lord. Is that what you prefer I use for you?" she asked, a smile creeping to her lips at his humour. She couldn't help it. Everything in her body stood primed and ready, as if she'd spent her life training for this one, single moment in time. She felt it was destined for her, and the heated prickling of her skin was just delightful.

Her voice was kind and subservient, and she had to do very little to alter it for him, yet there was a new genuineness that hadn't been there before. In all her years serving her princess, she had never shown such an honest desire to serve.

She had seen the wide array of women the dark God-King had at his disposal, but it hadn't deterred her. Perhaps he somehow recognized this, her curiously unique nature in that she was not intimidated in the face of his power. Where others saw something to fear and loathe, she saw potential for herself.

His charcoal dark face gazed down at her, soaking her in and piercing her all at once before his authoritative voice broke the spell of silence again. "The princess," he said, pointing towards the passed out woman without looking in her direction, "is she alright?" he asked, ignoring the woman's previous question, for now at least.

"One of the heads on the pike used to belong to someone she knew, though I cannot speak to her being all right, My Lord. I am trying to help her through this time, though it's troubling for someone as pampered as she." Mirella's voice was even and respectful, her manner forthright as she gazed over his body. She tried not to be so wanton, but it was difficult. How long had it been since she'd seen even a mortal in all his glory?

She swallowed and dabbed her pink tongue to the bottom of her lip, "She is not used to serving another."

Knelt as she was, it made it easy to gaze up at his impressive package, that bulge which contained his loins so massive through the black leather of his pants. The statue had done him little disservice in its representation of what lay beneath, but to be so close to the actual thing...

"I wouldn't imagine, no," he intoned thoughtfully.

Taking his time mulling over something he looked back down at her. "You will suffice," he stated, with a wave of his hand he gestured for her to follow. He went to the tent flap, exiting in a pace that seemed relaxed for him, but was brisk for her shorter limbs.

Excitement spurred her on, however, and she had no issue keeping up with his pace. She stayed a step and a half behind him and just to the side at all times, trailing him like she had so many others before, ready to aid him and yet giving him total control over all.

"My Lord, is it true that the others will have free reign with me when we finish?" she asked, his acceptance of her brightening her entire face despite the dark thought.

One unmistakable thing was that this time, unlike her arrival to the tent, the savages at his command not only averted their eyes, they were all prone before him. The first to notice his exiting his tent had set off a wave of like action, and as they re-entered the palace, it was uncanny. Never before had she seen such frightful obedience in all her years serving the royal family.

The old King had obedience, but nothing so deeply rooted as this.

Taking a different route through the ruins of the palace he spoke to her sparingly, "Your future remains to be seen," he stated simply. She had trouble guessing where he was leading her. When finally they emerged out onto a small garden area, reserved for the royal families' quiet breakfasts overlooking the city, she noticed the place was better composed than the rest.

The flowers were untrampled, the gazebo still stood. It was like a quiet center of the storm about the palace, untouched by the fury of the northerners. There he stood, magnificent but so oddly out of place, as he felt out of place wherever he was, like a being from another plane of existence.

Her eyes moved around, and her shoulders relaxed as they arrived, "I'm glad you ordered this place untouched," she murmured as she took a daring step nearer to the strange, godlike man with his otherworldly form. She was a fair bit shorter than he, though she was fairly tall for a lady. Her eyes twinkled with perverse delight at being alone with him, yet her heart raced with fear and desire, the two emotions whorling together and becoming one.

Though she hadn't been so frightened and cowed as the others, she knew what that hefty shaft could do to her, and her stomach turned in excitement as she dropped once more to her knees. Her hands reached for him, then faltered, "Do you prefer to tell me what you'd wish of me, My Lord?"

Her new dark king looked permanently consumed with matters of another realm, always seeming to be concerned with things beyond mere mortals understanding. Looking to her as she knelt before him, he took his time before answering. "You're a curious woman. You don't resist your fate at all, do you?" he asked, not seeming to expect an answer. He didn't seem to be used to carrying on conversations with women, or perhaps it was people, at all in fact.

"If my fate were unwelcome, I would resist. You are not unwelcome to me," she breathed, and he could see her chest rise and fall more rapidly beneath the burgundy gown.

"Are you used to serving like this?" he asked more meaningfully. "Did someone train you for a life on your knees before a man?" Despite his hard, husky words, she saw that hefty bulge twitch to life before her, the leather audibly straining as reacted to her.

"No, My Lord," she admitted. She had many lovers growing up, but none who were above her. None who deserved her. Her eyes dipped from his, trailing over his stomach and then further down, and she could swear her mouth was beginning to salivate in anticipation.

Studying the olive skinned servant, he took a step closer to her, lifting his hand from beneath his cloak and resting it upon her head. The man was so large her head seemed to fit in his palm snugly, and so strong and magnificently built, she would swear he could crush her skull if he wished.

"You have served your princess then as a servant," he stated rather than asked, "and not as the King's amusement or plaything." His heavy hand pet her sleek black hair, the weight of it pushing her towards his bulging loins until she was nearly pressed to it, the smell of leather and musk rich in her sinuses, and utterly pleasant.

"I never wished nor consented to serve a man in such a manner, My Lord, until I saw you." The words were completely genuine, and she shook a little as she said them. She wanted him, and she feared only that he would find her displeasing and send her away. She licked over her pinkened lips, "I am malleable to your whims, and be taught to please you best." Her desire made the words come out as a begged request as her green eyes met his, feeling so safe in his monstrous hand.

If he wished her dead, then she would only be pleased it was at a god's hands.

Perhaps if she thought with a clear head, she would realize how extreme her reaction to this man was, but there was no such moment of pause to escape the reality of kneeling before a God-King of the north.

Licking along his own full lips, the dark man brought his free hand to the gap between them, his fingers undoing some strap as he spoke, "You're a brazen woman," he stated firmly. "None of the Ka'reem" —a term for the northern savages nobody within Ariste had previously cared to use for the barbarians—"would dare speak to me so blatantly as you have. And none of the weak southerners can muster more than screams or cowering."

With the strap undone, his leather audibly groaned as it gave way to his heated flesh. The tension unfurled, his heavy cock toppled free, its shaft gloriously long and hard, thick veins ribbing its length as it struck her face, contrasting so darkly against her.

Her gasp was one of appreciation and as that heavy slab of masculinity rested against her flesh, her lashes fluttered down. "If I displease you, I will correct my behaviour," she promised, and her dainty fingers worked to his cock, grasping him and getting a feel for his size and heft. "I would kill my own mother to be able to gratify and breed for you. It would be the greatest honour," she muttered, barely even hearing herself any longer as her fingers pushed back his foreskin, her eyes riveted to that thick, otherworldly cock.

Never had she seen one so large and perfectly sculpted, and if she had ever doubted his godliness, it was completely disappeared now. He was perfect.

The dark man's brows raised as he watched her reverentially stroke his shaft. He was surprised, and it showed, for he didn't appear to be a man who was often caught off guard.

Slowly he resumed stroking her hair, "You'd do that willingly. Breed me an heir without complaint," though his voice was so dark and husky, she could detect that slight hint of surprise lining his words. "Other women are offered up to me, but even they cringe in fear of me. Fear what they shall birth, no matter how much their loved ones talk of the honour and privilege."

"Then they don't understand the honour of breeding a demi-god, My Lord," she purred, and the way she caressed his cock against the soft flesh of her cheek spoke so much affection and devotion. She still hadn't licked it, but she worshiped that pillar of strength with such adoring touches.

"If they don't understand the privilege, then they are too daft to be worthy of you," she rubbed him against her jaw and a light tress of hair grazed against his divine flesh. "I am not worthy of you, but I wish for your child to be."

Virile as he was, her words and caresses made the giant give a low growl of desire. It sounded divine from him, darkly divine. It was the first crack in his composed veneer she'd yet to see, and it was from stoking desire in him for her.

His strong fingers curled in her hair, taking hold of her head by the dark strands and with the ease of his might began to rub her cheek against his heated shaft even further. "It is a shame you weren't the princess," he mused gruffly, that hard voice of his lower, more seductive as she watched his glorious muscles swell and rise with his increased breathing.

Her own breath was baited as she revelled in it all, in his touch, in the feel of his flesh as it moved against her and filled her with such need. She had never felt anything close to this before, and her lip trembled with the power of her lust. "I'm sorry she will not serve you well. She will cry, and complain, and to break her will be lovely but it will not be a challenge."

Those words elicited a brief chuckle of amusement from the ebon giant, and he pushed her face down further, until she was nestled beneath that shaft, his hefty balls pressed to her chin. Releasing her from his hold he stroked her hair again, the morning breeze washing over them both as she knelt before him. "You are no noble born, that much is obvious."

"I do not care for pride and useless people," she said, her lips grazing against the flesh at the base of the cock, and she found it impossible to resist any longer. Her motions were so small and tentative, but fuelled by lust and need of an intensity she had never felt before. Her breath was a sweet wash over his member as her tongue pressed out, grazing across his skin.

She moaned at the first taste of his flesh, and she writhed beneath him, getting closer as his cock throbbed atop her face. It was undignified, but she cared not for such concerns. She just wanted to please her god.

With a light intake of breath, her tongue had an effect upon him. That thick shaft twitched and the mighty lord throbbed against her face. But a day ago she was a middle-aged servant to a prissy princess; today she was a concubine to a God-King that seemed to appreciate her efforts at least more than her former mistress had.

Breathing heavily, he watched her every little motion as she lavished his manhood with her affections. "Neither do I," he said at last, his voice heavy with desire.

Her mouth began to join her tongue, kissing against him as her lips tried to encompass the circumference of his hard, aroused cock. Every vein she traveled to its conclusion, and he could tell she was doing nothing to speed his way to his end. Whereas others might, in their fear and loathing, be hurried for his cum, she was taking her time.

Her concern for his pleasure, and her need for him to enjoy outweighed all. Her hands and mouth worked in tandem to feel out those glorious, pulsing veins and the soft flesh that covered the iron hardness of his cock. "If I were smarter, perhaps I would fear what you could do to me with such a weapon," she purred, but her words were nothing short of ecstatic. "Instead, the desire kept burning in me through the night. If I am not at my best, I apologize. Thoughts of you..." she moaned and shut herself up by curling her tongue along the shaft of his cock.

His harsh breathing grown so heavy, he yanked her face off his cock from its worship, his mouth open, his lips glossy from having licked at them with his hunger. "Show me your flesh," he commanded of her, those thick courtly servants robes now a distasteful hindrance from letting the mighty God-King see her in her fullness.

Her fingers worked diligently and it was only a moment before the heavy material slipped back from her shoulders and pooled at her feet. She was suddenly grateful for the quick trip she had taken back in the Princess' room to shed herself of her undergarments. She had understood all too readily what would be expected of her, and her firm, feminine curves were revealed to his hungry eyes.

She stood unmoving, encouraging him to look at her, to stare at the weight of her breasts and the light brown nipples peaked atop them, and the light bit of black hair that shielded her sex from him. Her curves were prominent and her hips were ample, as if made to bare his children. Her hand moved to her hair and removing a couple of the pins, she let the silky, black strands down around her olive shoulders, the straight tresses laid delicately atop her aroused breasts. Her hair was down to the middle of her back, yet she ensured that none of it hid her body from him.

"I can only dream that I please you, despite my lowly status. But then, we are all lowly compared to you, *My* Lord. Even that is too good for us, as it denotes our ownership of you. Your Greatness," she sighed as her eyes fell, "Shall I turn for you?"

Something she had said or done, or perhaps it was just her beauty, set him off.

The giant barbarian warlord grabbed for her, took hold of her neck and pulled her in as he lunged down, pushing a hard kiss to her mouth. It was such a passionate embrace of their lips, and the heat of his manhood jabbed in against her stomach as he forced his tongue into her mouth so deeply.

With a hungry growl he broke their kiss and took hold of her by her hip. "Your sweet words hide a sweeter form," he husked to her with almost venomous desire. The hungry man pushed her back towards the soapstone table upon which the royal family had eaten so many breakfasts over the years, pressing her against it so that she had to rest back on its cool stone surface.

Her skin excited with the sudden change in temperatures, his heated form at her front, and the cold rock on her back. She was so malleable and eager for him, and it only grew with his increased passion for her. Arms wrapping about him, her lips lunged for him again, even as her legs spread, that large phallus sending that combination of delight and fear through her.

She had never wanted pain so bad.

"To please you is a joy greater than I've known," she gasped before her tongue explored his demonic mouth, her need growing with every pulse of that great shaft.

Women offered themselves and were offered to him, but she could sense that such willing desire was new and different to him. It was a wholly new experience for the God-King that commanded fear beyond respect or obedience.

Pushing back on her shoulder, he made her rest beneath him upon the cool soapstone table. She had served her stuck up princess her meal here but a day ago upon that intricately carved surface. How things did change.

Looking over her voluptuous form, those heavy breasts that rested against her chest, the wide hips and pleading thighs, he rested his gaze against her slick slit to see the proof of her arousal. "You'll get your wish," he promised, watching as her slender fingers took hold of his unearthly heft and guided his manhood to her flower. The tenderness of that moment making him groan with desire even before he jabbed his hips forward and impaled the doting servant on his godlike ebon shaft.

She screamed, but it wasn't the usual sound of protest and hurt. It was something so deep and primal, and a hissed 'yes!' trailed beneath it. Her thick thighs wrapped against his hips, but she could scarcely accommodate all of his length, despite her desire and the intense arousal that made her body easier to plumb.

He was so deep within her canal, and the sensation was too much for her to bear. Though she had never been easy to bring to such pleasure—countless men had tried and failed, despite their diligence—all it took was the simple, single thrust of her new god's cock to send her pivoting over the edge.

He felt the way her cunny spasmed, the muscles contracting and massaging him so delightfully, but her cries and squirms were almost sweeter still. Her shoulders shifted, and with them, her breasts tilted to the side, the heavy orbs resting against her bicep before she jerked back against the table. Her back arched as the waves of ecstasy seemed to continue for an eternity.

When finally she managed to still her twitching form, she was still posed so near to the edge that her eyes watered as her hips began to grind him, "I'm sorry you can't fit, Your Greatness!'

The giant of a man had brought many a woman to screams and orgasms upon the end of his massive cock, but never before had he done so with such relative ease. Never with a woman being so willing and wanting. To feel her quake in unmistakable pleasure around his girth, coating him with such a thick rush of honey was satisfying beyond measure.

Resting a palm against the stone table beside her, he slid the other up over her, felt her large breast then teased her neck before stroking her cheek. It was hard not to appreciate the contrast of his dark cock against her olive skin, that thick trunk-like shaft of his prying her labia so wide, stretching them painfully about his veiny shaft.

"It'll do," he said in a quiet husk, moving his hand from the table to grip her hip and beginning to control her so forcefully as he rammed himself into her.

Even had he been gentle, it would have been a harsh experience, but the dark God-King spared her nothing as he began to piston his powerful hips, savaging her cunt with his dick as he grunted in pleasure. The look of rising satisfaction on his broad, handsome face such a thing of beauty, his long black hair dangled about him as he pounded harder, faster. They filled the garden with the sounds of flesh thudding against flesh.

She tried to look at him, to watch him tear her asunder and appreciate her body, but each new wave of pleasure sent her reeling. It took her another few seconds to recover, only to feel her body betray her inner thoughts to the man again and again. She was greedy to see him, but with each new orgasm, her mind hazed over further and further until finally she just lay with her eyes closed, letting her body respond naturally to the powerful thrusts.

Her breathing and moaning never stopped, and she couldn't stop her compliments from flooding past her mouth, and even her pain sounded exquisite as she shrieked and groaned beneath him. "I will care for your heir, make him strong and powerful, yet he'll never be like you. He'll be born of someone less than you and never rival your throne, but he'll terrify his enemies as you do," she moaned out, and her pleasure would not stop her praise. Her pain wouldn't hinder her from giving him what he needed, and she willed her body to open and blossom for the man, to give him what he needed.

It was with a quaking fury that the brute of a man hammered into her with a final, earth shaking cry, ramming his wide crowned cock into her depths and let loose his seed. With his strong fingers dug into her hip and breast, his hips twitched as he ground himself against her womb, the thick flood of his seed burning out of him and into her as he lost control.

It was excruciating for her, the way he battered her cervix with each new slap, but the satisfaction on his face as he unleashed himself inside her was all she could have hoped for.

The whole of his charcoal dark skin was coated in a sheen of light perspiration, making his hard muscles stand out all the more. She looked down, seeing his enormous cock sticking out of her so lewdly, begin to ooze the thick cream of his cum. Panting lightly, the large man's heavy breaths were of pure satisfaction, the act being nowhere near enough exertion to tire his muscular form.

With a lick of his lips he looked over her form with lidded eyes. "You've a breeder's body," he confirmed, "and the mindset to go with it, if you speak true." It was only then he loosened his grip on her breast, which drew attention to just how hard he had grabbed at her.

She felt the absence of his hand, and yearned for the aching pain once more, but instead she laid back, breathing desperately as she tried to regain her composure. She'd lost count of how many orgasms she'd had atop his great cock, but was grateful for every last one.

"Lying to you would be a carnal sin," she gasped, as if insulted to think she could do such a thing. Her green eyes worked up his body, but they only made it halfway before they dipped back down, staring at him as he impaled her, seeing the lips pulled so tight over his shaft. She wanted to say it to his face, but she simply couldn't stop looking at the lewd scene.

"Your Greatness, My Lord," she breathed out reverentially. "Please reserve me for yourself. If one of those... lessers impregnated me before you, I couldn't live with myself. I could be of such better use to only you." Though something told her it was already too late for that, that virile god had planted his seed and no man would supplant it.

The giant, dark man licked around his lips. He had curious, almond-shaped eyes that were a bit narrowed usually, and his jaw was chiselled and hard. He was such a curious blend of human masculine beauty and dark ethereal majesty it was hard to place anything about him specifically as he watched her.

"By custom," he began, his pecs still swelling with each new intake of breath, "I would hand you over to the troops to be used until they grew tired of you, or you were worn out." The ominous nature of his words were amplified by his harsh, gravelly voice. "And if you survived a birth to show a child of my breeding, you would be rewarded."

He was a cunning man, and he watched her through narrowed eyes, studying her in the silence after his declaration.

Her lips fell apart and her eyes reluctantly rose to his, a slow smirk coming to her lips, "I would expect no less from a cunning god," she spoke with such reverence. Her thighs were still so tightly pressed to him, the fleshy, sensitive insides held against his hips, angling herself back to try to trap all of the cum she could within the deepest recesses of her form.

"I defer to you, Your Greatness, but I cannot promise I will serve them well. My body belongs to another, and it would withhold their assaults until I could be returned to my rightful owner."

Trailing his hand up her form he cupped her jaw line, his thumb stroking along her lower lip where she tasted it there, suckling diligently as he spoke. "The princess," he began, "if she were mine... willingly mine... I would have a legitimate claim to the throne that none could contend with," he said huskily, suggestiveness rich on his voice.

There was the smallest hint of distaste at his

words, but it quickly made way for thoughtfulness. Her hands held his wrists, massaging his palm as she withdrew his thumb from her plush mouth, "Her father is dead, Your Greatness?"

Instead of pulling from her, the mighty man kept his cock hilted inside her slick cunt and lowered his hard body down atop her. His weight of pure muscle and bone could've crushed her, but he kept it enough to merely pin her with a delightful ache. "I split him open myself," he husked, his face so near to her now it let Mirella truly appreciate his dark, masculine beauty fully.

It excited her, his words, his closeness, his weight, and he watched as she swooned beneath him for a second before she swallowed. "Keep me with her. Keep us for yourself, and I will teach her what it means to be a concubine to a god. All I do will be for your benefit," she swore, and there was no begging to her tone. No neediness.

Though she desired to please him, she would do so in any manner he saw fit, and would not presume to tell him his business. If he chose for her to be passed around like a doll, she would be the best damn doll that those men ever fucked.

Perhaps it was that desire to please, or perhaps it was instead her willingness to barter for her position so cunningly, but it made his mighty shaft twitch within her quim, showing signs of renewed life. "If you do this for me," he began, licking his lower lip, "I will keep you in my harem until she is mine willingly. I will give you all that time to bear the fruit of my loins. And should you succeed before then, I will keep you to myself all the same." It was almost romantic the tone of his dark voice, talking to her so closely as they still lay entangled. "Help trick her into being mine, and there will be rewards for you beyond measure."

As close as he was to her, he could feel the beat of her heart quicken, and the muscles in her pussy clenched him tightly, though as large as he was, she needn't work hard. "I will not disappoint you, for I know the punishments will be greater still."

Rolling his hips, the thick, veiny shaft pulled out, then pushed back in. The soft suckling of her cum and honey glazed folds gripped him so tightly. He began to pump himself into her again, his cock stirring back to fullness. "Time is of the essence," he husked, the slap of his balls against her ass resounding in the courtyard as his pace quickened and he took her yet again upon the table.

Once more he silenced rational thought with a haze of pleasure, and she was back to compliments, instead. Pretty, truthful words that only rang more genuine as her hips moved against him and her thighs lifted her up. She cried as he hit against her inner barrier, but it didn't matter. Nothing mattered but for him and his awesome power.

# CHAPTER 3

Returned to the tent by one of the concubine-guards, Mirella had spent the evening tending to the delicate, needful princess. The morning didn't seem like it would hold much different.

New food was placed out for the women of the tent, and despite the odd mix it seemed obvious they were treated well, or so was the intention while there. In the span of that one evening she'd seen a few of the women taken and replaced, presumably to serve the needs of the God-King, but he hadn't shown up again, regrettably.

Plucking at some of the food on the manor platters, the princess whined, "This is awful." The food, though from the palace's kitchens, was not prepared to the standards the delicate woman was accustomed to.

"Come, now, Princess. It's not that bad," she popped another bit of melon in her mouth, chewing it and smiling, the entire act like the condescending way one speaks to a child. "See? Besides, you need your strength, my lovely girl. You need to be strong and fit so that you can get through these days."

Mirella had been watching everything with an excruciating attention to detail, noting which women were taken, how long they were gone, and everything about their demeanour before and after. She had a keen eye for intrigue, and she took it upon herself to be aware of potential competition or threats.

Only one of the taken women had returned thus far, a brown haired local with curly locks, she had the wide-eyed look of someone stunned upon returning and had kept to herself since. Her competition seemed less spirited than herself, she had to confess.

The princess, however, had spirit. It was just of the wrong sort. "Father will be here soon," she told herself stubbornly, the waifish princess refusing to eat. "Those... brutes," she said, gesturing towards the tall concubine-soldiers that were their guards, "tried telling me he was dead," and the refusal to believe it was strong with her.

She had thought on it for the entire night, wondering if she could break the princess and remould her into something fresh and better, or if she should use that naive hope against her. Mirella hadn't come to a proper conclusion. She licked her lips, "Princess, he would not like to see you starved and abused, too weak to stand on your own feet because of your refusal to eat." She plucked up some honeyed fruit, pressing it towards the woman and taking on a sterner tone, "Eat."

With a scowl the petite princess finally gave in and took a small morsel of food. It had taken all morning to get that much done and once swallowed—with great distaste—she seemed disinclined to eat more. "What's going to become of me, Mirella?" she huffed with despair, her slender shoulders sagging.

"You'll always be a great Princess, my lady. Always. Even here, among these beasts, they recognize your status and you'll be treated well. They won't hurt you as long as you don't make trouble for them." Her hand stroked along the woman's cheek, "I'm trying to help you. To make a deal with that g— the leader," she quickly corrected herself to a more amiable term.

Lifting her watery blue eyes up to her servant, the delicate princess stared at her with wide wonder, "Make a deal?" Slowly distaste filled her features, "Is that what you were doing yesterday when I awoke and you were gone? Consorting with the enemy?" The young woman's voice trembled in anger, disbelief and doubt.

"For you. To try to get you free and safe and back to your family," she said calmly, though she forced a twinge of hurt to her tone. "We can't fight, Princess. We're captured, and if we're not careful, terrible things might happen to us. To you. I can't allow that to happen."

There was obviously some conflict within her, the trembling, pale little woman lowering her eyes and darting them about in frustration. "That's no excuse to... to barter with the devil!" she exclaimed in a breathy voice.

This was all too much to handle for the young woman who'd only once been beyond the city itself, and then simply to be betrothed to her future husband, a prince of the Empire. Swallowing down her rage she asked, "What have you done, Mirella?"

"I've only looked out for your best interests, my lady. You are my Princess, and I only ever want what is best for you," she responded, obedience in her tone. "I'm only sorry that you had to wake alone. I so wanted to be there to ensure you were feeling well."

She seemed so sincere and downtrodden to be accused of such things, and her green eyes fell demurely.

The virginal princess could hardly wrap her mind about what had actually happened, and it seemed apparent she was struggling with the reality of it all. "I need some time to think," she said, though before anything more could be said that familiar sound of people falling to their knees could be heard behind them.

His was a presence felt before it was seen, and so Mirella was able to turn in time to see the grand, dark man sweep into the tent. Once again, where others cowered or bowed, she gazed up longingly.

Her gaze was returned, for the large tyrant approached them both. His dark gaze moved to the princess however, eying her quivering little form. "Good morning, princess Flair," came his dusky voice, so hard and masculine, using her official title for the first time.

Mirella had to pull her eyes from him, using all her will to look back to the Princess, stroking the backs of her fingers against her lady's hand. "Princess, please," she murmured softly. She wanted the praise of her god, and if she could only warp the princess to his will...

Why did she have to be so obstinate? Why did her father spoil her so? Mirella shoved aside the rage, her light caresses so encouraging, "He can help you."

The princess didn't flinch from her touch, which was a good sign, but she still remained cowering from the visage of the mighty giant towering over them.

"You needn't fear me, princess," he intoned evenly in that booming voice of his that seemed incapable of doing anything but commanding attention.

The princess, however, snapped then, "My father will come and save me! I don't need you or anyone to take care of me until then!" Obstinately she pushed away Mirella's consoling hand and rose up on shaky limbs, resolutely defiant in her ignorance of reality.

"Princess!" she gasped as she stood on far more certain feet. "You'll be no good to anyone if you get yourself injured," she murmured, leaning in to the other woman's ear, "Be rational," she pleaded.

Stumbling upon the cushions that lined the floor as she pushed Mirella away, Anabelle tried to escape them both but toppled onto a mound of velvet and silk, crying as she tried to separate herself from them both. "Leave me alone!" she cried. Mirella knew that tone of voice well, there would be no consoling the princess now, not until she had sobbed herself clean of her worries.

However, the greatest disappointment was the look on the ebon God-King's face. He said no more, but he chose two other women then, leaving her there to wait out the sobs of the petulant princess.

# CHAPTER 4

After hours of crying and pouting, Mirella's anger had plenty of time to boil. Despite her calming and matronly tone, her rage at disappointing her god, at being denied him was the most intense emotion she had ever felt.

At the palace, the Princess's moods like this could go on for weeks at a time on occasion. Here, under such dramatic circumstances, she feared for how stubborn she could be. Sleep claimed her eventually, and in the midst of the night the concubine-guards came to her in quiet, shifting through the dim, candle lit tent to rouse the handmaid from her rest.

There were no words, just a quiet look. Either it was ominous or they merely wished to not wake the sleeping princess.

She was a light sleeper at the best of times and disentangled herself from the sleeping princess, whose deep sleep was difficult to rouse her from at the best of times. Mirella primped as she followed them back the familiar route to the breakfast nook, and her heart beat with excitement and fear.

Surely he couldn't have expected her to win over the princess so quickly. Perhaps if she had informed the woman of her dead father, to have instigated her rage sooner, she could have moved the process along quicker. Her footsteps were fast and she nearly outpaced the guards as she sought to see her god and bare her punishment for failure.

Mirella found the man standing beneath the moonlight in almost nothing. The guard had not dared follow her in, and so she was left alone with the visage of her new idol, his dark, hard body seeming to glow in the moonlight. It took her awhile to realize he was glistening with some light perspiration as he stood there in his boots and pants only.

Turning around he looked to her passively, and his words shook reality, "She is a stubborn one." So simple.

"Yes, Your Greatness," she sighed as she moved towards him, her fingers working the ribbon of her dressing gown and leaving it partially open down the front. It was quite brazen, of course, but it was done with such a natural ease that it didn't seem crass.

"I'm considering if her father's death will help or hinder your progress with her," she was no longer speaking to him, but to his body, her eyes working their way over his form. There was no jealousy to her, no lamenting why he continued on with other concubines. She accepted him as is and was only grateful for time alone with him once more.

She swore she could hear that familiar groan of leather as his manhood swelled within his pants again. The dark lord reached out and took her in his hands, held her shoulder and hip as he looked down over her body with such masculine desire. "You can bend her to me," he intoned darkly, and it was only reassuring.

"I will, Your Greatness. If there is any one thing I will do in this world, it will be to see you happy," she murmured. Her softer body yielded towards him as her material gathered around his wrist, revealing more of her feminine form. She swallowed as her heartbeat quickened, and she wanted him so badly. To see him happy with her. To be the one he visited more than any other.

"The Princess is headstrong, but easily led. She will take her time to be emotional, but she trusts me. I will make sure she makes the right choice for you," she tilted her head up, looking over his muscled chest before finally meeting his eyes.

Brushing his hand over her cheek, he let the dress fall to the grass while his other hand stroked across her hip to one of her generous breasts. Standing so close to him, the swell of his manhood through his pants pressed against her, and she knew he wanted her. "Tell me, what can I do to soften her heart in the meantime. Will this stubborn princess be swayed by trinkets? Favours?"

He spoke of the other woman, but as he lowered

and tilted his head, he seemed focussed only on her. He was consumed with desire for her as he supped at the flesh of her neck, kissing, suckling and biting her there.

"If you've spared some of her friends, it might be a relief, depending on how supportive they are of you. To gain good will," she murmured as her hands pressed against his chest, feeling out his flesh so desirably. "Clothing, amenities. A bedroom. Things the princess wants. Return her life to as close as normalcy, and she will have an easier time processing this. Your men destroyed most of the things she put value into, and it is making her more stubborn than usual," she purred out. One of her hands swept over the bulge in his pants and she trembled with need.

She leaned in, brushing her lips against his ribs, tracing them so hungrily as she kissed his flesh, rubbing his manhood with growing speed and pressure.

The depth of her advice, the cunning of it, seemed to please the giant of a man at least as much as her touches. "Then I shall do that," he said with certainty. "I shall put her back in her room, restore things as best as can be done..." he stroked her sleek, dark hair, cupped and squeezed her large breast, appreciated the beauty of her voluptuous form in its totality. "But none of her friends likely live. The court had to be eliminated, to make way for my reign," he insisted, throbbing against her touch so thickly. "You are the only friend she can have."

She smiled as her fingers found that sweet release of his pants, plucking his throbbing shaft from its confines with such relish. "I don't know why that should please me, but it does," she said as her fist began to worshipfully massage his member. "Certainly it isn't that I enjoy her company, but to have her rely upon only me..." her grin widened. "Besides, those pissants deserved to die."

Her harsh words about the dead nobles seemed to bring a toothy smile to his face, and he looked down at her as she began to pump his massive shaft in the night air. The roll of his foreskin exposed the thick bulging ridge of his crown, and a husky growl of pleasure brewed from within his chest.

"You're mine," he stated possessively, his fingers knitted into her hair as he stroked her head. "Will it help your cause if she thinks you were responsible for negotiating these new arrangements? Or would it be more beneficial to me to take credit for my gifts?" he asked as his powerful hand, coarse and strong, kneaded her breast flesh, teased and toyed with her areola and stiff nipple.

She thought about it, or at the very least tried. Her mind was quickly beginning to give way to a haze of delight at his hands, his hardness throbbing against her palms. "Take credit," she murmured. "The Princess must see you as her 'saviour Prince'. I'm but a lowly handmaiden," she purred. It sounded so incredibly selfless, but the deviousness was obvious.

Her body ached for him and that distracting wetness between her thighs grew as she massaged his member. Again there was no intent for him to cum, just a pure enjoyment of feeling him in all of his glory.

Leaning down, the obsidian giant plushly placed a kiss against her pouty lips. "You know your place well," he husked so complimentary, "how can I meet with you without raising the Princess's suspicions? I need your reports," he stated, his voice hanging for just a moment before he squeezed her breast painfully hard, "I want your flesh." Despite his magnificence, his power, when he spoke in that lust laden voice, it had a way of making her feel like all the world had fallen away and she was the sole object of his desire.

"She sleeps well, Your Greatness," she whispered against his lips. "I need little sleep to be rested, and I would do without for months if it meant more time with you." She swallowed hard, her hand and her stomach trapping his cock in the heated embrace of her flesh, her large breasts pressed against him as if encouraging his hard squeezes. The way she moaned with each new pain seemed to demonstrate her joy quite well.

With his hand in her hair and upon her chest, he twisted her around. To be manhandled by a god as she was bent over, pushed down so that she had to rest her hands against the soapstone table where he'd first taken her.

"You serve well," he husked as he brought his thick pillar to her quim, the slickness of her cunny kissing the bulbous crown. "If you fail to produce me an heir, I shall be saddened by that." He stabbed himself into her, forcing that thick girth to the very base of her quim and yet still more of his length unable to fit.

She braced herself and for only a second she

wondered if this was where he took the other women before all thought and reason left her. All that was left was that aching fullness, that needy, hard cock as it battered into her from a new angle, sending familiar tendrils of ecstasy up and down her form. Though she didn't cum right away as she had last time, her pussy tightened around that gigantic member, her breasts flattened atop the cold table and the sensation teasing her higher.

This time was rougher, harder, and more primal than the first. It was as if in the pale moonlight this beast of a king was fuelled in his dark desires. He held her generous hips in place, keeping her from moving too far from his hold as he pounded her from behind. If this was the kind of treatment he gave other women, there was no wonder as to why they looked so blown away after their encounters with him.

The hard, dull thuds of his iron cock shaft impacting her depths were each a new reminder of the throbbing pain she'd carry from this experience long afterwards. The slap of his heavy balls against her sodden clit and mons like a mocking clap in the dark of night. But the sweet sounds of husky male satisfaction were delicious enough to make up for it, especially as she felt his member swell and the flood of thick virile seed to follow.

She huffed against his force, and she wasn't even entirely sure if she had yet cum herself. She had certainly felt pleasure coalesce within her body, but he had taken her to a place she'd never been before. Somewhere beyond mortal needs and flesh. Somewhere within herself and yet outside of all reality at the same time. When she felt him release within her, it grounded her instantly and all that otherworldly experience had her body shuddering around him with an intensity she didn't know possible.

Panting over top of her, he stroked his fingers down her spine, eliciting a trill of excitement as his cock throbbed and disgorged the last of its virile seed into her eager cunt. "If only the princess were as agreeable and pleasing to me as you," he remarked. A hand squeezed her ass cheek before he pulled out of her, leaving a void within that only a man as impressively large as he could ever hope to fill.

Her hand instantly went down, cupping herself and hoping not to drop a single glob, though it was a fruitless thing. It poured over her fingertips, both of their juices leaving her hands sticky and slippery in the dim light. "I wish so too, if only to better aid you," she sighed, genuine desire hidden in her lust laden voice.

Placing a hand on her cheek, he guided the servant up and tilted her gaze to him as the pair stood in the grove, her legs wobbly after the hard fucking. "Find a way to fulfill my wishes, and you shall be lucky compared to her in the end, sweet concubine," he promised, and then a thought seemed to take him. "What is your name?"

"Mirella, Your Greatness," she whispered. It was as though she'd been utterly humbled, and his asking for her name was the greatest gift she could have been offered, even more so than the rutting that had left her weak and dizzied. Gratitude flooded her body and she wanted, even more so, to please her god.

His hand released hold of her head and he stroked back over her dark hair, "Mirella," he repeated, as if tasting her name upon his tongue experimentally and liking it. "Go back to your charge, Mirella. And dream of a day when you no longer tend to prickly princesses, but are mother to warlord princes."

She bowed, but her eyes never left him, still so eager for him even as she limped back, feeling the exquisite ache so deep within her, hand still lovingly cupping her sex and her robe haphazardly closed around her.

# CHAPTER 5

Mirella awoke to an odd sound. The princess had somehow awaked before her and was talking to someone else in the tent. She could only attribute it to the late nights spent serving the God-King. Those moments were so deeply satisfying, but they had a way of leaving her exhausted the next day, of course.

"Those savages couldn't have defeated us fairly," declared Anabelle. "They don't even have a real army!" The petite little princess was speaking to three of the other concubines, women of Ariste who—in their new scanty little outfits—seemed more amenable to their leader's speech, nodding along. "The King is out there somewhere. Don't listen to the lies! Our soldiers will return home and liberate us."

Before Mirella could intervene, one of the northerners responded in her stead. "We may not have the sort of army you once had, little woman," declared a short haired barbarian, "but we have our own special ways. And the God-King knows best how to use them," she said, down casting her eyes at the mention of their leader.

Outrage and insult flooded Mirella's face, but she quickly swept it aside, once more hiding her true feelings under a mask of calm. "My Princess, war is never fair, but if your father were alive, he hasn't come back for us."

That denial sent Anabelle's expression into a state of shock. Her eyes wide in disbelief at Mirella's 'outrageous' assertion, she looked ready to either break down into tears or attack the servant. "How dare you," she muttered with barely any force to her words. The petite princess struck out with a slap, her weak wrist able to do little more than inflict a mild stinging at her insolent servant.

She made it seem like it hurt a lot more, her hand clasping her jaw as her eyes widened, "Princess!" she gasped. "It's obvious to any here! His daughter is in danger—the Princess!—and yet he's done nothing to save you from your lot! We're surrounded by the dead! I only want what is best for you, my lady, to see you protected and safe, and if your father will not, then I will!"

She saw from the fire in Anabelle's eyes that her words would not sink in just yet, however. The princess was too full of indignations rage to see the reason of her 'false' words.

Before things could escalate further, however, He returned.

A hush consumed the room, and as the God-King strode in he had a smile. A light smile, "Princess," he addressed Anabelle, "I have come bearing good tidings for you." The look on Anabelle's disturbed and repulsed face almost seemed to betray hope for a moment.

"What tidings could YOU bring me that would be good?" she said scornfully, making her reference to him sound insulting by itself.

She took a step back away from the Princess, embarrassed at having been caught so with the Anabelle. She would hang that little bitch herself if she didn't submit to the god soon. Her rage dissipated, however, as her eyes scanned him greedily, and her desire to make the Princess his rose.

Dressed in his usual attire, the cloak draped diagonally across his exquisitely sculpted torso, he looked as stunning as ever, his immaculate hair so rich and lustrous in its dark glory.

"I've arranged for you to return to your rooms in the palace," he said. "You can go back to living there, with my blessing and some tokens of my affection." It was generous of him, "And in addition," he gestured to Mirella, making her heart stop, "you can have your servant with you."

It was all so perfect, then Anabelle spat on it, "You can't buy me off!" She nearly shrieked. Her obstinacy knew no bounds as she stood and clenched her fists. "I will go back to my rooms alone to await the King!" she declared, storming around the God-King and being caught by two of the guard-concubines. He waved them off, and they let her go, instead escorting her on ahead into the palace as he lingered to look to Mirella with a hint of confusion on his handsome, broad face.

Shame broiled through her, and for the first time, her eyes dropped away from his body and towards the floor, "The Princess is upset. I will speak with her in the morning." She'd pushed too far, too hard. It'd been too much. She cursed herself at her failure.

# CHAPTER 6

The next day, Mirella was informed the princess refused to see her by one of the guard-concubines who was beginning to show sign of pregnancy, her tummy having swollen just slightly. It was a crushing thing, so much depended on pleasing her new King, and the Princess's tantrum could go on and on, as she very well knew.

Worse yet, he hadn't sent for her that night. The women of the concubine's tent were antsy; they seemed to sense something was going on as the guard informed the servant. "His majesty is on his way here, I'm told. Be ready," it was more of a general remark, to all the women, however, rather than being reserved simply for her.

She was always ready. Though her rage still bubbled, she knew this could be a good thing. To have the Princess isolated, for him to be her only point of contact could work favourably, and she was filled with confidence in her new plan, or so she had thought until the announcement came. She didn't expect him to pick her, not really. The punishment was grave, but so was her disappointment, yet still she stood ready.

She had become far more comfortable with her body and had taken on a general state of semi-undress. There were skimpy outfits, free for the taking, and though she had worn her robe earlier when refused by the Princess, here in the concubine tent, she had no such shame. Most of her body was visible, the top barely holding her ample breasts, and the skirt hardly hiding anything as it went on an angle down her thigh. She pulled her long, black hair off her chest to leave it looking more vulnerable to his eyes and held her breath.

The women who persisted now were more of the type who feared and gave in to him, mixed with fewer of the new ones. They still cowered and looked bewildered by it all, their pale Aristean features contorted in alarm.

When he entered all of them looked away however. All but her. For that she was rewarded by a twinkle of interest in his gaze as he saw her, dressed not in her servant's robes, but as a true concubine and pleasure slave. The light material of her outfit barely covered her at all.

The worry of the night melted away as he came to her out of them all. "You look much better like this," he remarked in his heavy tone, the compliment so sweet coming from the ruler of everything from the Aristean Mountains on northwards. His hand reaching out and helping itself to touch her stomach, squeeze a breast, all openly and without reservation.

She had the same lack of concern as him. They were nothing to her, less than nothing. Not even her equals. They were nothing but walking wombs to her, and she nearly lost her breath as she moved in against him so readily. She only hesitated for a moment, wondering who among the traitors to the god might tell his Princess. Mirella leaned up, whispering her concerns only to him, "None who see us should be allowed to speak with the little one."

Her caution made him smile, and it was such a sight to see. It wasn't the fake little thing he gave for the princess not long ago, this was genuine. And it was for her.

Leaning down he murmured to her in his husky voice, "Too right." It was nothing, just two words, but something about how the dark God-King bent and said them to her and her alone amidst a sea of stunning women made her feel so special and unique.

With his free hand he undid his cloak and let it fall to the floor, his gaze sweeping about the room, taking in all the other women. "Since the princess is gone," all measure of quiet conspiracy gone from his voice, "it is due time I took a moment to visit with my harem."

Topless and stunning, the large man strode over the cushions, his hand leaving Mirella's breast but moving to her shoulder, guiding her along with him so that she was at his side. It was his guard-concubine, the pregnant one again, that spoke up. "It is a privilege and honour to bear the God-King's children. His seed must spread far and wide," she intoned it as if it were some litany of prayer.

Mirella's breathing quickened, and he could see dark delight begin to spread on her face as she moved with him. She didn't care much for the sterile manner the woman praised her god, but it was a far sight better than the cowering, weak willed and useless women of the city, so her smile broadened. "Too right you are," she said with awe and respect. "I can only hope I will prove as useful to him," she moved her hands down over his body brazenly, and her voice rose, "We are being offered something so few ever receive. It's no time for fright or uselessness. Instead, take time to pay your respects to one so far superior to us all!"

A rousing speech, for her first time, she thought as her hands worked down over his abs and thighs.

Her obedient praising, her fawning touches, it seemed to earn her a low, growling groan of approval from the giant man, dressed only in his black leather breeches and boots. Stopping near the center of the chamber, his powerful arm around Mirella, he studied the new women a moment before looking to the pregnant guard-concubine. "You've done well. However I think for this time I shall let the privilege fall to the new one," and his hand slid down Mirella's back to squeeze one of her sumptuous ass cheeks, indicating his favour.

The guard-concubine retreated, not daring to show any annoyance at being passed over as she slid away to the entrance. Mirella was now the favoured one, and the God-King looked down to her, "Pick the first one. It's your duty to help spread my seed to the far corners this day, Mirella." He blessed her with that familiar use of her name, his groping hand still palming her ass cheek.

Her smile was mostly hidden beneath her pensive gaze as she sought for someone pleasing. They all looked so pitiful and cowering and frightened to her, none of them filled with the admiration and respect they should have, not even after her rousing speech. Her eyes fell to the one that wished the greatest not to be seen, however.

A small woman, she was young and ripe, with her nearly white hair and her peach coloured flesh. Mirella almost felt as if she wanted to taste her then and there, and her lips touched to her god's lips as she whispered to him, "Do you prefer them ready for you, Your Greatness?"

Helping her stand up to whisper to him by pushing up on her round backside, he murmured back to her with a slightly wry smile. "If they aren't ready, then it falls to you to either make them ready, or slicken me with mouth or quim to compensate, pet."

He uttered those words so darkly, but the twinkle in his eyes showed great amusement at her question, her eagerness to please. With a hard squeeze and a slap of her olive toned ass he said, "I trust you shall choose right."

She wanted to do both, and for a moment she seemed so torn before she slipped away from him, reluctantly, and walked to the other woman. She was sat upon some of the pillows and startled as Mirella arrived, but that kind, genuine smile on the olive skinned woman's face was so reassuring. The peach skinned beauty had trouble speaking but stammered out, "Don't let him hurt me."

Mirella nodded, her hand presumptively going to the other woman's arm, "He won't. He just wants to watch us enjoy each other," she lied so easily. It didn't even matter that he'd just been speaking about concubines and that she'd given an impassioned plea for everyone to let him fuck them. Now it was all sugar, and her hand ran down the slender woman's body, "You're very pretty. So slim and perky," she said, and the way she was knelt before her, the skirt fell away to the side, exposing her large rear to the god behind her.

He watched with rapt attention, his eyes lidded as the former handmaiden worked her ways upon the pretty young woman. Her choice seemed to please him, despite the nervous Aristean's diminutive size, so similar to that of the princess with her dainty figure.

Where she stoked the fires of the reluctant woman, he pulled off one boot, then the other, slowly removing what little clothes he had left on.

Her actions were so slow and calculating as the woman shivered beneath her touch, and Mirella gently guided her face with her finger so that they stared at one another.

"Tell me, my sweet. What is your name?" Mirella breathed.

"R-Rachel," she managed back, her stutter pronounced as Mirella smiled brightly.

"That's a beautiful name for an absolutely beautiful woman," she said before her lips grazed the other woman's, the action so slight and delicate it seemed completely contrary to the hard, desperate desire she'd shown for her god. "I'm going to kiss you," she punctuated the word with another peck to that peach skin, "and he's going to watch, and it will all be okay. Have you a lover, Rachel?"

"N-no!" she gasped squirming away, but Mirella stopped her with a firm hand to her slender thigh.

"Just relax," she cooed, her green eyes working lustily over the woman's body. Already her own arousal was growing, despite her usual disinterest in women. She didn't get along well with them; they all reminded her too much of the Princess. Full of themselves and with such an ego. They were all so much better than the lowly handmaiden, but here she had the upper hand.

Even as she teased and toyed with the pretty young woman, she could hear the familiar groan of leather as her new and only King shed his pants; the peel of that dark material from his thick muscles as he freed himself of all his clothing. He stood there in pure male glory with his thick cock so prominent and large.

Rachel trembled; she wore very little, though it was obvious from her nervousness that it wasn't by her own choice. The slinky outfit consisted of but three triangles of transparent white cloth over her two breasts and slit, and did nothing to hide the colour of her sex beneath. The cloth was rimmed in silver that came to chains which bound it together about her waist, ass and back. It seemed to be a style that pleased the God-King, for it was given in abundance in many different styles to the concubines.

She had rejected it for that reason. She had no interest in dressing like the others, and as her skirt fell way to show her pantiless behind, her sex visible as she bowed before the other woman, she could only hope he enjoyed it even better. As her hands trailed down Rachel's body, the thumbs grazed the lines of her panties, warming her to her touch so gently.

"This will feel good," she promised. She had become an expert at strumming her own body to new heights after being with so many inept men in the past. She only hoped that this woman would be responsive as her head dipped, her nose running along her slit as she inhaled deeply.

Rachel cried out in alarm and tried to shift back once more, but those hands on her thighs tightened. "Would you hold her still, Your Greatness?" she asked, the hot breath flooding over the woman's sex.

There was a gasp and a murmur from the entrance to the tent, and she knew then that the guard-concubines found her presumption at asking their deity for help an affront. Despite that however, the powerful man was there, upon one knee as he pinned Rachel down with immense ease. She could barely squirm beneath his strong grasp as those charcoal hands pinned her shoulders and arms.

The smell of that giant man, his musk of arousal so near, was intoxicating, and she thought she could even detect a shiver of lust pass through the blonde woman as well.

She nuzzled that woman's sex, trying to ignore the object of her interests so near to her, and her eyes focused instead on that young woman. She was probably over a decade younger than herself, just around the marrying age, and even though Mirella hated her for her youth, she loved the scent of her clean pussy.

Slowly she peeled away the transparent fabric, and that first touch of hot tongue against her hotter sex was sublime. The taste was beyond compare, and Mirella moaned quite genuinely into the woman's cunny.

The shuddering mewl that came from the young woman betrayed her enjoyment. Despite being pinned beneath the grasp of the obsidian warlord, and having cunnilingus forced upon her, she quaked and quivered.

Before long the woman's moans grew pleasured and her body lost its tenseness, enough so that her lord took one hand off Rachel and brought it to her own black hair, stroking along it in tender approval.

She didn't want to stop. She didn't want to do anything but bring this woman to the pleasured brink, and even as her jaw ached and her mouth began to go numb, her tongue whipped across her clit with more enthusiasm. Her own breathing was coming on hard and fast, especially under the touch of her god, and his being there made it all the better.

Sharing the woman with him, bringing her to such heights as she was pinned between his hard cock and her beautiful mouth was just exquisite. She had never anticipated that she would enjoy something so tawdry as this, but she knew then that she would gladly do this and far more for just the smallest amount of approval from him.

It was almost disappointing to feel him nudge her out of the way, ending her delving into that young, pink pussy. But when she saw the swell of that unearthly cock, its veins so prominent and dark, and the look of longing lust on his face that would brook no further delay, she saw it for what it was. It was reward for having done her duty so very well.

With one dark hand on the pale woman's shoulder, he pinned her to the cushions as he slid over top of her. That heavy shaft of his bobbed upwards, and he hesitated for just a moment. Enough to let her realize her duty and so she reached in, lifting its large heft and guiding him in towards that damp flower. She let it kiss his dark crown so lovingly before he began to push down into that virginal slit.

Mirella licked around her mouth and still tasted the other woman's sex so strong on her lips. She wanted to see, and even that jealousy could do little to hinder her enjoyment of this. Instead, she wormed her way up along Rachel's side and watched the fear and desire mark her face.

"It will hurt, but it will be delightful," she promised. Her hand worked down between the two, pressing roughly against that aching, pulsing nub between her nether lips. She worked it expertly and caused the younger woman to gasp and moan, her legs parting wider for that unearthly cock.

With a depth of approval she had not expected, her king leaned in and kissed at her lips, pushing his tongue into Mirella's mouth. The embrace of mouths went on long until his shredding of Rachel's innocence on the head of his cock brought the young woman to a shriek, and he broke it to look at the pale young woman, not ceasing his dive as he plumbed the depths of that virginally tight quim, bottoming out within her and immediately beginning to pump pitilessly.

She was breathless, and the shared taste of the woman between them was something so primal to her. Fingers working faster between those saliva and honey soaked lips; she moved to silence Rachel's cries, but only for a second. She just wanted enough to share that sensation with her as well before moving onto her neck, sucking her tender, peach flesh almost brutally as her god fucked the other woman ruthlessly.

The slap of his dark sac against Rachel's pale ass grew, his husky grunts and groans creating a stir in the air as he pumped himself faster, harder. As Mirella worked the young woman to a frenzy she saw the throbs in his thick cock widen that torn slit, the labia stretched in a completely vulgar display.

With the tightness of that quim and his ruthless pace, it wasn't long before she saw as her lord and master worked himself to his release. With his handsome face contorted, brows knitted, he groaned loudly as he buried himself into the young woman and emptied his loins of all their virile cum, utterly filling that poor girl with his seed.

Jealousy once more edged into her mind, and she became so aware of that painful throbbing between her own legs. She'd never wanted someone so bad, to ever devote herself to one person's pleasure so selflessly that she'd deny herself, but she knew it was good. It was what he wanted, and even though she hated the idea of Rachel or the other concubines spawning his child, her hand worked its way up to the woman's stomach, rubbing it gently.

"You are so lucky," she breathed out with such wanting.

Rising up from Rachel's pale, quivering form, he slid out of her reddened slit then grabbed for Mirella. The action was so fast, so abrupt, he seemed angry. Those strong arms took hold of her, and he pushed her away from the young woman, moving with her so that she and her God-King rolled down a pile of cushions together.

When they came to a halt he had his arms about her, their bodies pressed and he was forcing such a passionate kiss onto her. What had seemed like violent rage at first became clear to them all as some depraved act of lust or affection. With his slick, stiff cock jammed against Mirella, he ground against her and kissed her so deep, so passionately.

She was at a loss and that haze of lust overwhelmed her. Arms flung around his neck, she met each one of the presses of his hips with her own. She was so wet that she felt it down her inner thighs, unhampered by panties, and the skirt had easily fallen away, revealing her lower half to the room full of half-naked women. She didn't care about them, though, nor the tiny mewls of pain from Rachel at her side.

Instead it was just him, just her, grinding and kissing in the quickly warming tent.

When he finally broke their kiss, it was to arch his spine and raise his shoulders, gliding that thick, meaty shaft down along her slit until he was positioned to nudge it into her. He was insatiable, like no other man she'd been with nor heard tale of, and he had his cock within her and was thrusting and pumping like some mad animal in heat.

It was more than the intensity of it, the passion of it. The way he was positioned over her so, it was dominance. It was possessiveness. He was claiming her, marking her as his in front of all the other women. This wasn't about breeding, this was about much more, she could tell that as she glimpsed across his glossy chest and watched him pound her long and hard into the rich cushions below.

The tiny, peppered moans were silenced against his lips, again and again as she sought to press as much of her flesh to his. Relief and need mingled within her body as she licked and bit at his neck and chest, gasping and panting as her legs spread wider, his hard, charcoal coloured cock splitting her pretty little lips open again and again.

The sight was so crude, but for them, it was perfection.

When she felt that familiar swell within him, his pounding having brought her over the edge and into screaming pleasure, he reached out, grabbing another woman by the ankle and yanking her strongly towards them.

She couldn't tell if the other woman resisted, though being one of the new ones she found it hard to imagine she wouldn't. And instead of the pleasing rush of her king's release inside her, she felt him pull out. Immediately he tanked another brunette to him, impaling her on his cock with a brutal thrust. He paid no heed to her lack of readiness as he jack hammered his final moments out to a roaring climax.

She gasped and instinctively rolled towards him, her body following after his even as he denied her that finale. Her body shuddered and shook with the aftershocks, but still she wanted more, even though she felt so sore. So very sore. It didn't matter though. Not even the fact that he hadn't given her what she wanted mattered.

All that mattered was that he got what he wanted.

With a snap of his fingers he kissed Mirella hard, panting and breathing heavily as he yanked his cock from another seeded cunt, pointing to a new woman. "That one," he instructed, his hard pecs rising and falling so dramatically with his heavy breathing, making him look like a living statue carved from obsidian.

# CHAPTER 7

The princess was being stubborn. So very stubborn. Well over a month of insistent sulking and refusing to meet with her trusted servant. Not that it displeased Mirella on a personal level. Being away from her meant she was almost like a queen of the concubines. It was her that the God-King trusted to select his women for fertilization. It was her he showed obvious favouritism towards.

Most importantly, she hadn't had a period since he'd first taken her, and the aching swell of her breasts both suggested she was quickened by his seed.

The only damper on it at all was the knowledge that her lord had grander plans that relied on the Princess's cooperation. And that was still not forthcoming.

When the summons came to her, the guard-concubines brought her through the palace, but to an unusual place. It was a back viewing hall, rarely used by the old king. It had a series of wide windows that viewed out through the gap in the mountain pass to the green fields south of the mountains. There she found the throne, torn from the very marble floor of the throne room and placed overlooking the plains south.

In his usual garb, sat the God-King himself, in some deep contemplation.

"Your Greatness?" she asked curiously as she made her way in. Already she'd disposed of her clothing and was so gloriously, triumphantly nude as she moved to his side. Her gaze was unable to move from his for a long few heartbeats before she finally followed his stare outside.

"Something troubles you?" she asked as she moved to his lap, quite brazenly sitting her firm rear atop his leather clad lap.

They were alone, and it was strange to be in such a massive hall accompanied only by the marble columns around them. He responded quite well to her approach, putting his arm around her, holding her close and taking no objection to her forward manner. She'd come to realize over the time since he'd taken over that he appreciated her brazenness. Mixed with her true devotion, it made a sweet nectar for the dark man. A true respite from everyone else with their fear and grovelling.

Stroking his hand along her hip and waist he kept his gaze through the mountain pass ahead. "The seer is coming," he stated simply, sounding troubled, rubbing his lower lip with his free hand before he placed it on her lap.

Her breath held, and her back pressed against his chest, "The Princess still sulks. I had hoped it would isolate her, leaving you to become her only point of contact, yet I've failed you," she lamented. "If only that fucking bitch would get over herself for ten seconds, I could have her be yours, I'm certain of it." She didn't sound whiny, but she was quite obviously disappointed in herself.

Sliding his dark gaze over to her it was like having her soul flayed. With a squeeze of her hip and thigh he took a deep breath, his chest expanding. "The seer would not be coming here unless it was urgent. More urgent than the fickle whims of a little princess."

His gaze passed down over her, her bare flesh distracting him, but only somewhat. She could still see the creases of worry on his broad face despite his attraction to her, despite the throb of a stirred cock beneath her round ass.

Her hand went to his face, trailing along him, seeking to work out the worried furrows and reassure him, "I'm only your servant, Your Greatness. I cannot hope to foresee things as you. What do you make of it?" she asked, her words so gentle and not at all condescending. She was absolutely genuine with him.

She had spent most of the months since the conquest in the concubine's tent, but on occasion he had taken her out, brought her to various places in the palace itself. Most often the breakfast grove, since she seemed to like it. But this was the first time he'd taken her aside merely for the pleasure of her company, it seemed. For even though he stirred to her, he didn't simply take her as he usually did.

"I fear events move quicker than I foresaw," he muttered in that dark, otherworldly voice of his. "I thought I would have over a year at least to secure my holdings before the Empire stirred. But if my mother—" he hesitated, as if he didn't mean to say that and regretted it, "the Seer comes, then it can only be to warn me of grave doom. She would not leave her hovel otherwise."

She spent a long while thinking on this. She hadn't great military prowess or knowledge, and her face contorted briefly. "If the King is dead, then it must be the Princess' betrothed bringing you trouble. He is the only one with a true vested interest," she said calmly. She always hungered for him, but she wouldn't dream of presuming upon him when troubled so. Instead she just continued to stroke him, her fingers working along his muscles.

Taking a deep breath, he reclined, shutting his eyes as her olive toned fingers strummed over his muscles, soothing away his worries. She comforted him. It was such a realization, to acknowledge that her king—her god—found comfort and relief by her mere presence and touch.

"You're wise," he said at last, opening his eyes to narrow slits and looking at her. "But if you're right, and a prince of the empire marches against me, I haven't the men to stand against them." His grip on her tightened, painfully so, for just a heartbeat, but he relaxed. "Retreat might be the only option. To leave behind the city and its spoils."

She rubbed him so gently as she thought that over, her head shaking in protest, "This is yours. The city and its spoils belong to you, and I won't let you lose that. I may have failed with the Princess, but I will not fail in this. There is a way," she nuzzled his jaw. "We will think of something."

Her bold words surprised him, and he furrowed his brows again as he looked to her, studying her as if she were a new person altogether.

It was a long silence of his studied gaze, only broken when he lifted his hand, stroking his fingertips along her stomach, then breast. He pressed his palm to her darkened areola and squeezed, the tender, swollen mound aching with the pain of it before he released. "You're pregnant," he said simply.

"Yes," she responded in the same, clipped tone, but her smile was undeniable. Her fingers ran along his jaw, teasing him before returning to tend to the muscles in his neck and shoulders. "And I will give birth in the same place I conceived. This is your domain, now, Your Greatness. We will fight for you," she paused, licking her lips. "One of the others," she said, obviously referring to the concubines, for whom else was there, for her? "They mentioned they have certain powers you can best take advantage of. Would you grace me with their battle knowledge?"

She had seen nobody but the other concubines and him for so long, there was no mistaking who she meant. The suggestion made him arch his brow and look on at her in surprise again. She was full of intrigue.

Licking along his own full lips, he squeezed her against his hard body. "The women of the Ka'reem are forbidden to fight. It has been so for time immemorial," he stated this plainly, "until I came along." But she could tell on his voice there was something else. Something he wasn't saying but seemed to beg to be pried out of him.

Her lips found his neck, and her breath washed over his throat before she kissed him, the light sensation so tender and doting. "But?" she whispered, her smooth skin rubbing along his as she nuzzled his ear with her nose. Her fingers still worked against him and she was a constant source of pleasure with the way her expert ministrations worked him.

With a husky groan he squeezed his thick bicep about her, mashing those heavy, engorged breasts to his pecs. Biting her ear, he ground his arousal against her, stroking a hand along her full hip as he muttered lowly. "You are a vexing woman, Mirella. A dangerous plaything," he remarked with every bit of complement his voice could hold.

"It is a secret. Even amongst the Ka'reem themselves." He hesitated, his breathing heavy, "It is why the men fear their women without even knowing why."

A brief huff of air passed his flesh, a half-hearted laugh with a quirked grin, "I thought it was just because they were tough." Her hands kept finding all those right places, playing him so expertly even in this new situation. Her tongue traced along his

Adam's apple, suctioning around it for a second before she pulled back, her green eyes on his.

"I am yours, Your Greatness. In all things. Let me help you and share your burdens," she pleaded, so genuinely.

It was no easy decision. That much was obvious watching his smooth, unblemished face contort in thought over the question. Sliding a hand over her stomach, he pressed in against it, feeling the slight bit of hardness beneath her soft, smooth skin, as if feeling evidence of her pregnant state confirmed something for him he needed to know.

With a stern nod he said, "You'll meet the seer. She'll judge you. Perhaps teach you," he remarked. Then added softer, "I hope she finds you worthy, as I have."

She felt so tender at his touch, but his words drove her to a place she'd never known existed within herself. She fought back the signs of her weakness, but that moisture remained in her eyes even as she tried to blink it back, "What should I do? How will she judge me?"

He saw her weakness, those dark eyes of his broke through her barriers and saw the softness within her despite her attempts to hide it.

"I don't know," his lack of knowledge obviously bothering him. "As I have said, these are matters of the Ka'reem women." He reached up, brushing some of her sleek black hair from her face, leaning in and kissing her forehead. "I understand them better than any man alive, yet I do not have the answer to either question. You shall just have to show you are better than your birth."

She nodded, but there was something stuck in her throat that she struggled to swallow down, her lips pressing against his so flushly. "I will do it for you," she murmured against his mouth, her nose pressing against his as she shifted, her swollen breasts flattened against his muscular chest. "How long do I have? And how shall I dress?"

"Days," he responded to the first, but had a slight smirk for the latter. "It does not matter. The seer does not see what is. Only what will be. Or was." He kissed her lips then, the sound of their moist mouths smacking resonating in the massive, empty hall.

He throbbed beneath her needfully, and he finished, "Now do your duty for your king. I must think." His hand moved through her hair, taking hold of her head and pushing it down in so blatantly suggestive a manner she could hardly miss it.

As always, she was only too willing. She shifted into position before her teeth tugged at the binds that held him. Her hands and mouth sought him out as he sat atop that throne, stewing about the future. She, too, had matters on her mind, but the moment that throbbing shaft pulsed against her wet mouth, they all slipped away in favour of better things.

# CHAPTER 8

The Seer's arrival took longer than anticipated. It was a week of anxious waiting, though during it Mirella had managed to grow closer with one of the guard-concubines. Svella, as she came to learn her name, was a tall, voluptuous woman that looked fearsome at most times. Even with her bare belly swollen, pregnancy having sunk its teeth into her rather fully, she looked like nobody to trifle with.

In some ways she was similar to Mirella herself; her devotion was no less true to the God-King, though it was not like hers. Nobodies could be, she determined.

Sat with her legs crossed, the pale Svella, with her dark hair braided down around her shoulder, dressed only in boots and loincloth, told her tales of the north. "Our people once rode the fields of the south, many long ages ago. We were strong and rich. Now," she shrugged her strong shoulders, "it is that which taunts us. Boils in the veins of so many Ka'reem. That we sat in weak hovels in the north, cold and hungry, while the little straw-necks lived large."

Mirella was dressed in a casual strip of material that just barely hid her engorged breasts and showed off her large ass as it pressed against one of the pillows. "No one could blame that," she agreed, her forced casualness obvious, even to a less observant woman than Svella. She braided her hair against her shoulder, undoing the twists and redoing them, just to keep from fidgeting more obviously. "Once your numbers grow, you'll be a force to reckon with once more."

With a haughty laugh the large woman gave her a look over that Mirella could've taken as open hostility if she hadn't gotten to know the woman over the past months. "We already are. The God-King has taught us we are greater than any other force," she stated with full certainty. "He brought to our fighters the cunning we lacked. Now we are unstoppable," she stated with a broad smile that showed her conviction.

Therein lay the difference between the two women. Svella was absolutely dedicated to her lord, but only because she saw him as the saviour of her people. The embodiment of her people.

Mirella smiled, her lips quirked so pleasantly as she observed the other woman. By rights she should see her as competition, but both were swollen and both served their god in their own ways. She was as close to a friend as she could manage in this place, and she accepted it willingly. She was a damn spot brighter than the Princess, anyway. Besides, Svella never held it against her that she'd supplanted her as the God-King's favourite.

"Well, then, imagine when your numbers do swell. It'll be overkill and then some," she teased, looking quite excited for the prospect.

It was strange. The numbers of the concubines never decreased, but almost none of them were familiar to Mirella now. Aside from the Ka'reem guards, she was the only woman allowed to stay on after it became apparent she was pregnant. The others got their 'freedom', or whatever it was that happened to them once taken away, the moment they showed signs of pregnancy.

Mirella was blessed. And the guards had come to accept she was special as well, albeit begrudgingly in most cases.

The new women from the city were always the same; beautiful, young, frightened. Their numbers always restocked, and Mirella had a hand in each of their deflowerings.

"I confess," Svella began, "I was jealous of you at first. You have the God-King's eyes," she made a symbol over her chest and downcast her eyes at the mention of His Majesty. "But you serve him better in such manners than I have or could," she stated with a sort of professional understanding. It was all duty for her.

"You have other things to focus on. I have him,

fully and utterly. We both serve, in our own ways." Mirella left it unspoken that her way was better, of course, though no woman could blame her for thinking it. "But thank you," she smiled at the other woman, her eyes scanning over her with a kind reverence. "He deserves to rule this land."

For Svella the notion of the God-King as a man and as an embodiment of a whole people was a dichotomy integral to her faith, but something she barely understood. All the same, she nodded and gave a light smile. They were so different, despite their unifying cause.

The moment was interrupted, however, by the sound of great horns and clamouring feet. There was commotion going on in the courtyard outside, but the horns and the sound of marching feet were definitely from the city proper below.

Svella stood up, "The Seer," she said, eyes wide, her voice full of awe and reverence. She'd gleaned little of the mystical Seer so far, not that the guards didn't want to talk about her, they did! But they held her in almost as much reverence as the God-King himself, and when in a group were always afraid to speak of her at any length for fear of embarrassment.

Moving to the tent flap she pulled it open, shameless about her near nudity. Mirella had not been confined to the tent for some time, or at least, she didn't suppose so. Though she had contented herself with her Master's will, coming at his whim or staying otherwise. When everything she could want was provided to her where she was, she had little reason to wander off.

She didn't bother fretting about her outfit—or lack of one—and simply rose. He had enjoyed her brazenness, but she had no real understanding if this woman would. She knew it was important and dared not to disappoint, so her back straightened and she mustered all the courage she could as she slipped past the tent's entrance, standing outside in the glaring natural light. Her body was on display with her large, pregnant breasts spilling forth from the two strips of fabric that hid little more than her nipples, the dark areolas visible.

No other concubine but her or the guards could have wandered off like that, but the two went to the walls of the palace courtyard and climbed the stairs. The few men who were still there moved away, giving them a wide berth. Though both were obviously pregnant with the God-King's children, and they could not have supplanted that seed, there was still a tremendous taboo on being anywhere near his chosen women.

Leaning upon the intricately carved walls, Svella looked out over the city below. The winding roadway that curled up the hillside through the buildings towards the palace was designed for defence. It meant a party such as the grand procession approaching the cities gates would take almost an hour to reach them.

"There she is," uttered Svella with awe in her voice, eyes wide with shimmering marvel.

She didn't feel the same awe, though she wondered if she should. The mother of a god... She wondered at that frequently over the course of the week, but still her mind hadn't wrapped around it.

The man—the god—she knew had no need for such things. She still had issues coming to terms with it, and as her stomach pressed against the cold stone she was transported, just for a moment, back to the garden.

She shivered as she looked towards Svella's gaze, trying to capture that same look of respect on her face.

"How should I address her? What is she like?" Mirella murmured, moving instinctively closer to the other woman.

Svella could not tear her gaze away from the procession below. For the Ka'reem it was one of majesty and pomp, which as a people they were not fond of.

Large banners flew in the air, streaming in the winds from the north. It was hard to see them clearly from there, but Svella handed her an eye piece looted from the palace. "You do not address her," she stated in a subdued voice. "The Seer is no longer a woman... she is beyond us now," she explained.

Peering through the monocular she saw the guards, they were women, like the concubines. But they wore heavy armour, long cloaks of shimmering black flowed behind them, and the full face masks and helmets made them look like hideous, beaked monsters. She saw nothing of the seer however, for she must have rode in the palanquin at the heart of the procession, shielded from sight by silks.

Not a woman? The intrigue was getting to her as she stared over the procession, feeling suddenly so naked and vulnerable. It wasn't a feeling she enjoyed outside of the bedroom—or the garden, or the throne room—and she looked back to Svella, "What do they think of us?"

With a shrug of her shoulders Svella leaned on the parapet further. "It has been many generations since we have had a seer whom could pass on her foresight to the people. I have been in her presence, have performed ritual. But never has she spoken of or to me, if that is what you mean." She looked directly at Mirella, "Many women would kill you if they knew you were about to see her. Even in defiance of the God-King," she paid the deferment, "to keep our secrets safe."

"Oh." Well that was reassuring. She handed back the looking glass and her skin prickled with nervousness. "We should await them?" she asked, more than said. She was usually so calm and in control, but in this, she was looking to her lone ally.

Placing a hand reassuringly upon her shoulder, Svella gave her a reassuring smile, "Do not fret. If the God-King wishes it, it is for the best." She could not doubt the large woman's faith in her lord.

She smiled up at that woman so warmly, and felt real affection for her then. It was a beautiful moment, at least for her, and she kept close to her side. "The other girls don't realize how lucky they are. I wish we could show them."

Svella turned her gaze and quickly downcast her eyes. "If only we could," she said, and then nudged the other woman to look around. "Though some are more fortunate than others," she stated as she showed Mirella sight of the God-King himself, arrayed in his usual attire, with gloves and raven-helm on, which made him look more terrifying. "He wishes you to go to him."

She swallowed and squeezed the woman's hand before her bare feet guided her to him so readily. Despite it all, she had faith in his judgement. If the woman found her to be unworthy... she pushed the thought from her mind. She'd deal with that when the time came, and drew her shoulders back confidently.

Accepting her by his side, he waited stoically. It was a strange moment, to see the mighty man so quieted around her, but then she'd gotten use to her private moments with him, where he was more and more unleashed with her. His passions having become inflamed for the woman to remarkable heights.

Waiting for the procession to arrive, the horns grew louder, and when finally the guards came through the palace gates she saw their glittering black cloaks were made of raven's feathers. The banners fluttered above with a base of black, showing a depiction of a weeping bloodshot eye at its center.

Everyone was quiet but for the approaching group, and around her all the northern Ka'reem had their fists to their chests in salute, with their heads bowed quietly. The God-King's only response, however, was to turn and head into the palace itself, leaving her no choice but to follow.

Inside she saw the windows were shuttered, their stained glass blocked out and all the fires and people emptied, leaving only small candle flames to light the way. The guards continued their march until they had carried the palanquin inside, resting the ornate, shamanistic looking mobile-hut into the center of the chamber.

Then, with a clap of metal garbed fists to chain mail vests—a thunderous noise that reverberated through the halls and left the chamber quaking—the guards turned and exited, leaving only the two. And the quiet Seer's cloth and hide residence.

Mirella barely breathed, stood so near to him and in such a strangely unsexual manner, despite the fact that she wore bare strips of fabric that clung to her pregnant form. She was half a pace behind him and to his side, deferential to him as her green eyes remained on the tent.

Seemingly tired of waiting, he pulled back his helm and stepped forward, "Mother," he called forth, and the tent seemed to stir at last.

From out of the tent-like structure Mirella heard the first sounds of life. It was like a giggle taken by madness, drifting from out of some crack in the void. It made her skin crawl and she wanted to cower like all those women that fled in terror from the God-King.

Pulling open the front of the tent she saw her at last. It was not what she expected.

The woman inside, dressed in crimson robes that looked dyed in blood sat in a heap. She looked... off, that was all she could say.

Unlike her son, she shared the pale skin of the Ka'reem. Paler still than most of them. Her long hair was white and draped about her shoulders. In fact all colour seemed seeped from her entirely, and she looked limp, almost lifeless, swaying slightly as she sat. Though she was alive. And more than that, even in her condition, so obviously ill, or semi-conscious at best, she had a certain beauty about her. She might have been twice Mirella's age, and her features looked delicate in spite of her height. Even then, with her hair white, her skin so pale, and age having taken its toll, she was beautiful.

"Mother," he called to her again, pulling back the thick flap further as he sounded more impatient. "It's me," he said, those last two words sounding so kind and familiar, in a way she rarely heard him speak.

It made the old woman stir abruptly, her eyes opening and shown to be milky white all the way through. The seer was indeed blind. "Kulav?" she called weakly in the air, the voice so normal, so motherly, not at all like the mad laughter she heard before.

"Yes mother," he responded calmly. "You are here with me now."

Kulav. Mirella smiled a bit, as if she'd just received some wonderful gift, and yet here she stood at the brink of... what? Insanity? Madness? To see him with this aged woman, he felt so strangely mortal to her, and she wasn't entirely sure what to make of the sensation. Instead, she remained a pace behind her god, and plastered on a smile for the old, sightless woman.

The seemingly mad woman drifted off again, it was hard to tell what she knew of what was going on or not, as she seemed to sway out of awareness yet again.

"Mother, you came with important tidings," the God-King Kulav stated.

"No," she responded, "no tidings."

"Then why di—"

"Because you have need of me," she responded before he could finish.

With the raven mask pulled off his face, Mirella could see the mild frustration on his handsome, dark features. "Of course, mother. You've come to warn me of the Empire?"

The woman swayed to the side, seeming to fall over, but she held herself but a hairs breadth from the cushions of her seat. She laughed maniacally, that chill sound seeming to make all the candles about Mirella flicker and dim until the old woman was done. "Why would I come to warn you of that which you already know?" The words sounded mocking, but then she softened, and sat up again, a motherly tone to her voice, "My sweet Kulav."

For his part, the dark lord seemed to take this in stride, perhaps used to her ravings and lunacy, undaunted by the sense of foreboding that afflicted Mirella. "So the Empire is—"

"Don't play at being dumb, my sweet," she cut in again, "it doesn't fit you. You are far too clever for that." The mighty God-King managed to look mildly irritated by the words from the old woman. "Of course they come. You knew they would. You have long planned for an early arrival of their forces." She sang her next words in some bizarre, otherworldly tone, "It was always in the stars."

Mirella tried to edge out her own frustration.

This was worse than speaking with that delivery boy that couldn't say a single word without stuttering. She wondered at how this god before her ever managed to make any sense of it, though she was quickly becoming more casual in her stance. The fear at meeting the woman was dripping away the longer she had gone unnoticed, and instead she simply, silently, urged her on. For his sake. And her own, of course.

"Then I have the matter in hand?" the dark man asked, anxious for his answers, even if he hid it well; though not well enough to keep it from either of the other women.

The old Seer's head lolled about on its seemingly weak neck, that curtain of white hair flowing around her as she teetered from side to side. When he got no answer Kulav said, "That's not how things work," as if repeating her own words, though she'd said nothing, "of course."

With a sigh he looked about to speak again, but instead the old woman cut in, "I came for your pet," she stated, and Kulav looked to Mirella with only a brief delay. "Yes her," she responded, though her milky white eyes never moved, and she never lost her erratic, random swaying that at all times looked like she was about to pass out and die.

She let loose a piercing wail of mourning, "Though it means I can expect to see less of you still, my sweet, sweet boy. My lovely little child, my—" her long litany of cooing, doting terms went on but Kulav gestured for Mirella to approach.

Well that was unnerving. She moved forward

with little delay, her hands behind her back as she approached, leaving her pregnant stomach and swollen breasts thrust forward. "I'm here," she said with a soft, beguiling smile, her tone so rich and calm, despite the anxiety she felt within. She was an expert at hiding her emotions when she cared enough to, and she definitely cared enough to now.

Her words, however, never interrupted the woman's long incantation of mewling fondness for her son. It was only when he spoke up again that she ceased, "I do not have that kind of need of you any longer, mother," he stated firmly. "Now my needs are grander."

The old woman clucked her tongue and flailed violently for a moment. "Nothing is grander than you, my son!" she said, her arms for the first time moving, hands raising. "You have no idea what I must do for you!" She wailed in agony once more, her slender fingers and long nailed digging into the side of her head as she seemed to be in mortal agony.

"Mother? Mother!" he called, leaning over and touching her arm to try and stop her from hurting herself. The mere contact seemed to bring her back to lucidity.

"She carries your blood in her now," she stated with extreme clarity. "She can be a witch of the coven because of that."

Mirella's black brow arched, and she looked to her god quickly. A lot of women carried his blood now, many with her direct influence and help. He was, she'd noted quite readily, a very virile individual. "Your Greatness?" she asked curiously, uncertain of how to deal with his lunatic of a mother, uncertain of what she meant, and what this meant for her and them.

The towering God-King looked down at her, his own brows furrowed slightly as he flitted his gaze between the two women. The same curious glint was in his eyes, but before he could put them to voice the mad woman spoke again.

"She means it, you know? Truly means it," and the Seer was taken by another fit of mad laughter that seemed ready to consume her.

When their patience was nearly at an end and he started to turn, the Seer spoke once more in chilling calm. "When you march to war again, bring her to me. Bring them all to me," then she fainted. Her robes flapping as she just unceremoniously fell into a pile on the cushions.

The hard-faced Kulav recognized it for what it was, he bent over the palanquin, kissing the old woman tenderly on the forehead and restored her carriage flaps.

Guiding Mirella to the back stairs, rather than to the front doors, he explained simply "That's all she has," leaving her for her own raven-guards to collect, she presumed.

"Oh," Mirella murmured. She had been left dizzy and confused, and despite the fact that she always seemed to stay so close to him, she was almost overlapping him as they walked. Her breathing was a lot heavier, and she forced herself to calm down, but the confusion still swirled in her mind. "So that went well?"

# CHAPTER 9

Svella had once stated that it was considered an excessive waste—a sin even—for the God-King to spill his seed fruitlessly. So that meant he could not spare his virility for the pregnant of his harem. Since meeting with the demigod's seer-mother, he'd kept her with him instead of in the tent, and she'd wondered if she could get him to violate that taboo in private.

On her knees before him and between his legs as he sat by the window, she lavished his manhood with her affections as he sat nude, seeming to fluctuate between deep contemplation and appreciation for her and her ministrations.

The tower he was in gave a view of the mountain pass, and it was not favoured by the old rulers. The room itself, though large and opulent, would've been reserved for guests only, but he preferred it. His mind always on the next challenge beyond.

For the past few days, she'd been a constant around the palace, and was growing to like it more and more, despite the worries that plagued her. She wanted to be of more help and use to the god, but she could barely make sense of the woman's ranting. As her tongue ran up the base of his shaft, she played with him, enjoying his company immensely.

"Your Greatness?" she murmured softly, her kittenish tongue prodding him.

Through all his deep contemplations, she always managed to keep him so rock hard, that magnificent shaft never losing its rigidity. So when he looked down at her, its thick girth blocked out much of her face. "Mirella?" he responded in his husky tone, that organ throbbing, disgorging more of its slick precum from its dark, ebon-purple tip.

Her tongue swirled up to capture it. She took such pleasure in his body, it overrode everything else, "How do I become a witch of the coven?" Both of them had been lost in their own contemplations. As she worked him so skilfully, her green eyes peering at him from beneath the sizable shaft, her tongue poking out along the sides, she knew she needed more from him.

Taking a deep breath his broad chest swelled, those hard muscles, seemingly etched in stone, rising then falling as he peered back out the window. "Mother will see to it when I march off to meet the princes army," he said plainly, the obsidian king enjoying his time with her, seeming more relaxed than she'd saw him to be in ages. "I don't know more than that, I'm afraid."

He hesitated, licking his lips, "The Ka'reem men despise the might of the witches. And women in general," he explained. "They work mysterious magics that have effects beyond their understanding. But they more often refuse to use those powers. Regardless of the cost to the people. So," he shrugged his broad shoulders, "the men fear them for what they might do, but loathe them for having such strength over them and refusing to use it."

She was thoughtful for a long time as she worked that huge member, devoted to it. Though she still simply teased him, there was a quickened pace and a firmer pressure against the swollen tip. Her mouth suckled him so eagerly, not worried about the aching in her knees and the heaviness of her breasts. "Would I be the first non-Ka'reem woman practicing?"

Her increased efforts had their effect, she saw the tensing in his hard muscles, the lines of sinew rise for a moment before softening again from his neck on down across his pecs and abs to his thighs. "As far as I know," he said with lust in his voice, she'd gotten through his barriers, and she could tell his mind was no longer elsewhere. It was focussed on her.

"The witches don't share their secrets with any outsiders. Never have from what I managed to learn of them," he couldn't help but grunt a little, that monstrously large cock throbbing thickly as his heavy sac laid down between those powerful thighs of his. "Mother is no longer a wealth of information on such things however, not since..." he trailed off, shutting his eyes and reclining, enjoying her fellatio.

She wanted to pry, to find out why, but something more important occurred to her. Though her hand still stroked him, her fingers rubbing lightly along his sac, she tilted her face from around his cock, staring at him curiously. "Will this put something between us?"

Breathing more heavily he opened his eyes ever so slightly and looked down to her as if troubled that her mouth had ceased its movements on him. "You're willing to do anything for me, are you not?" it was less of a question and more of a statement, but he seemed to expect an answer nonetheless.

"Absolutely," she said, instantly cutting off further conversation by suckling him once more, seeming reassured by his words and eager to get back to pleasing him. If he wasn't concerned, then certainly there was no need for her to be. As her tongue whorled around him, her eyes were focused on his.

Watching her a while, she saw his mouth slowly fall open, his breathing grown heavier. "Come here," he told her in his harsh, lusty voice, pulling her arms to get her to sit in his lap. She rose up, bending her knees and lowering herself onto him. He held her hips and angled her so that his member slipped into her cunt, those puffy lips still so tight for his large size, making him groan in pleasure.

She leaned against him so eagerly, pressing her soft, nude form against his, her arms wrapped around his neck tightly. As her mouth found his, he could feel her intensity and desire, her need for him and his reassurance. When he'd found her all those months ago, she'd been so entranced by him and his power and coveted both.

Now, she had let herself fall open to him, to someone else, in a way that no other person had ever been able to even let her glimpse. He'd torn into her and made her utterly his, and that kiss, the way she fucked him was one of love. Of her love, of devotion and worship and praise.

Those strong hands of his felt out her body, kneaded and stroked those engorged breasts, brushed past her already budding stomach and then back around her to her ass. That powerful grip of his lifted her up and brought her crashing back down at a quickened pace, so that she was riding him hard.

Breaking their kiss he husked to her in his gravelly voice, "You'll serve me no matter what happens. If I come back defeated, and the witches sorcery has driven you mad, I'll grab you by the hair and drag you into the north to rut still."

Her laugh was soft, but he could tell there was real affection there, a tenderness shared between them in their own way. Her lips found his neck, then his ear, her voice whispering to him, "What happened to drive her mad?"

Her entire body was such a delight, and the way her hips rocked were so skilled, tailored just to him. Her entire behaviour and actions had all been fine-tuned by her god, and that gave her all the more confidence in them as her thighs pushed up and down with his grip.

The slight tensing in his body beneath her pumping form betrayed the sensitive nature of the topic, but she wasn't reprimanded. The harsh conqueror instead squeezed her ass cheeks and hurried her pace, sending her achingly engorged breasts bouncing and crashing against her chest with painful force.

He didn't answer her, not right away. Instead he let the moment go on, her sweet kisses upon his hard flesh helping coax him along. It was then she felt it, his inhuman girth twitching, the old familiar feeling as finally she brought the God-King back to climax within her, not having to share the moment with any other.

Instead his seed shot out into her—for her—alone, and he arched his neck back, pushing his head into the back of the chair. Her continued pumping squeezed the creamy essence out of him entirely, leaving him breathing hard, his glistening chest undulating.

"Do you really wish to know?" he asked, his voice not upset but calm.

Her body still sang from his climax, and her entire form trembled against him so tenderly. She loved him. Awareness of the truth crashed through her and left her weak. That familiar wetness began to slide from her tight quim, and she couldn't help but send a frenzied scurry of kisses up his neck to his lips.

When finally she came down from her high, it was only just enough to nod, her eyes intent upon him.

The God-King Kulav didn't get up, didn't disturb the peace of their moment. Instead he tightened his hold on her ass and pulled her in against him in a tight embrace.

He rested his head against the top of hers, forcing her to nestle in against his neck and chest beneath his chin, the final throbbing of his cock inside her tight quim the only thing to disturb the moment. "Mother didn't warn me against you. And she's agreed to show you secrets that could destroy us all. So I suppose it doesn't matter," he stated in a light act of surrender that acknowledged his trust in her.

She kissed him so tenderly, just enough to try to coax him along as she rest in his lap, feeling herself reach a state of calm and peace she'd never known existed. He was helping her transcend the barriers of reality, she was certain, for the way she felt about him surely could not be attained by a mere mortal.

With his lips so near to her ear, she seemed absorbed into his hard, gravely words, that masculine husk so entrancing it seemed to consume her. "They said my mother made a pact with the Lord of the Hells when she gave birth to me. Her husband disowned her, cast her out.

"She lived a life of miserable poverty. Beaten and abused by the others of her tribe. She was the object of their hatred and blame, for all their misfortune." His thickly muscled arms tightened about her just slightly, "As I grew older, and my dark visage grew more and more pronounced, they decided I had to be destroyed to save them from the curse of the devils.

"My mother," he hesitated, "would not allow it. She paid a price too heinous to mention to see me to my safety. A price she has never stopped paying, Mirella." His dark lips kissed along her ear for a brief pause in his telling, "When I returned, many long years later, a grown man... she was battered. Broken. Abused. A slave of a lowly battle-chief. I slayed him, claimed my mother as my own in the spoils of combat."

With a deep intake of breath that swelled his chest out and made her whole body rise he then sighed almost inaudibly. "She was still cogent then. But she was broken. Blind. She felt a burden to me" he rephrased, "she was a burden to me."

With a lick of his lips he hesitated once more, "She delved into powers of the coven on her own that not even a hundred witches should have. And she did it for me." He kissed along her cheek, and then tilted her head back, moving to her lips. "That is why she is as you see her now, and shall forever remain so."

Her breathing had stilled to the point that for a moment it seemed like she was asleep until that first bit of moisture hit his chest and he felt her eyelashes bat against him, her body beginning to tremble. Her clutch had grown on him and she nuzzled against his throat so tightly she feared she might cut off his breath, but it didn't matter. She needed to be against him, to be a part of him, and even though his cock still pressed to her, it wasn't enough to still her sobs.

# CHAPTER 10

Life as the God-King's favoured concubine was not an easy one. In the tent with the other women, Mirella had almost free reign to do as she wished, except for those times she was called to serve. Instead her day began early, for the warlord Kulav—as she'd come to know his true name—was a demanding and insatiable Master who awoke early, slept little and was ever busy.

He was glorious to see in action though. His ebon body so toned and muscular as he pounded into her from the break of dawn until his morning lusts were sated in her, leaving her a panting, wet mess, drooling his sacred seed.

Slipping from the bed he stood gloriously nude, his massive shaft still rigid as he prepared for the day. "Run and see that breakfast is brought up," he commanded in his gravely, early morning husk. "The usual for me," he instructed, "but for you: two eggs, a sausage, and a tundra-berry pancake with as much syrup as you like. Oh, and some tea for me, juice for you."

He was already assembling his usual attire, his long black hair pushed behind his shoulders, for once, as he read from some parchment arrayed on his dresser.

She never deviated from his orders, not in the slightest, and though she pulled on some pretty little underthings to please his eyes, she felt no shame of it. Of course a God would be more commanding than her prissy, stubborn princess, and she was grateful for it.

His orders, she understood. They weren't for his vanity, or to suit his whims. He had a purpose and she was joyous that he included her in them. When she returned, it was with one of his servants trailing her with his order, impeccably arranged, likely by her.

She nodded to the table, having him set everything up before retreating, a soft smile playing at her lips.

Dressed in his half kilt and boots, he moved to sit at his table, beginning to eat immediately. After he had already dug in he gestured to the other chair. "Sit. Eat," he said in his gruff voice. Those dark eyes of his studied her as she sat her increasingly pregnant form next to him. "Have the seamstress make you some new things today," he stated firmly.

She nodded with gratitude, beginning in on her

food more slowly and with great appreciation for both it, and his company. This was the life she was meant for, and she knew she would worship this man until her dying breath.

"Do you have anything in mind that you'd like to see?" she asked as she pulled her glossy black hair over her shoulder, exposing that long, olive neck.

She was in her thirties, far older than any of his other concubines, yet that never stopped his dark gaze from passing over her with such interest and desire. "Tell her to make you one of my usuals," he insisted, and she was reminded of the outfit all the others had to wear, "but add some of the raven's feathers to a circlet and gold chain. Then have her make you a loose gauzy robe. See-through," he explained, eating as he talked. "Adorned with more of my royal feathers."

She realized the significance in that. Only him and his elite guards, the ones who watched over his mother or protected him specifically, wore such raven's feathers on their garb. Her heart pounded in her chest and she swallowed a lump. It was too much of an honour, yet she knew not to question him. Instead her head dipped in reverence and gratitude.

"Your Greatness, you honour me," she breathed.

He had nothing more to say to her on that, and it wasn't until his breakfast was finished and he rose in his glorious majesty to grasp his cloak that he spoke again. "The princess has asked for you again," he said simply, pulling the garment around his shoulder, letting it drape over his arm as he looked down at her.

"I've told her it'll take some time to find you, as

you were cast out into the masses when she dismissed you." A slow smile formed on his face, "I trust you can use that to your advantage." He touched his heavy hand to her head. "Go see her once you've finished your tasks. Tread carefully."

Fear gripped her but she nodded, "I live to serve you." She needed to do this, to succeed where she had failed before, and her head leaned into his caress. "Thank you, Your Greatness." She knew his name. She knew his story.

It did nothing but make her respect for him grow, her determination to please him solidified.

With a nod to her he left, the business of a God-King never ending, she knew.

Her day went much as she was used to. A lifetime of serving a needy, whining princess or another noble had prepared her for keeping track of numerous tasks and managing it all in her limited time.

When the time came to visit the princess, she was able to find some old rags akin to what the troubled masses of the city below were forced to wear these days, and was ushered up to the princess' room.

Let in, she was struck by how perversely decadent it was. Even compared to before, this was over the top. The princess had been showered with gifts, all the riches of the land and beyond to win her affection.

Though seeing the slender, waif-like noble beauty come around from her balcony, the look of distaste on her face said it hadn't done its trick. "Mirella!" she said, eyes wide as she approached the woman. "Oh I am so sorry, I have missed you so dearly!" She said, the female guard shutting the door behind her and leaving them be.

Mirella hoped she looked stricken, the way she collapsed into the Princess' arms and let out a sob, "Princess!" She angled herself to press that pregnant orb into the thin woman, letting her feel the reality of what she'd let her servant become. "I'm so glad you're safe."

Even if she was trying to garner the Princess's sympathy, she realized the woman had little sympathy for those not herself and that feeding into the Princess' ego couldn't hurt. "It's been such a misery out there without you to lead us," she whimpered.

Anabelle looked stricken and touched at once, putting her thin, young arms about the older woman. "My poor Mirella," she cooed, "I am so so sorry..." And strangely enough she almost sounded it. Almost. "Come in and have a seat," she invited, leading her to sit at the little breakfast nook chair.

She stroked her former servant's dark hair away from her olive toned face, looking at her with sympathy. "I know this must have been so very hard on you," she said soothingly.

"I was just so worried. I had no way of knowing if you were safe. I'd heard such horrid rumours that you've stepped away from leading, that you have no interest in it but worse still was that I'd heard you'd been injured, ill. I almost died myself the day I heard you were pregnant. I was cast into such torture when I rebelled to try to see for myself," Mirella lied to the much younger woman with such ease.

The young, blue-eyed noble somehow managed to go even whiter with shock at the woman's words. "Pregnant?" she said with such scorn. She rose up and looked around with displeasure, "He's done everything to buy me off but resurrect the dead!" She said with exasperation then scoffed again, muttering distastefully, "Pregnant."

She spun back on Mirella and her eyes were alight. Somehow she'd kept her spirits up all this time here alone. "I'm saving myself for the prince, my betrothed," she said dreamily, looking as if she had something she wanted to say.

Slipping into the seat beside her, the princess lowered her voice, "I know you've been through awful misery, but you were the only one I could trust. And I needed someone in the city when the time came."

Mirella's head tilted to the side, her brows furrowing, "What is it you need, my Princess? I am forever at your service," she bowed her head in reverence to the other woman even as her stomach churned.

The princess took a deep breath and looked troubled. Speaking in such a careful whisper she seemed to fear someone overhearing them even then. "I had to stage our little... fuss to get you out there, Mirella. I knew I could trust you, only you, to be faithful without needing to be in on the plan. They... they have strange powers and insight I think, and would too likely see through our charade."

The dainty princess gave a hopeful smile,

reaching out and taking her servants hand, "You can forgive me... right?"

"My Princess, I'm honoured you trust me so," she said as her eyes watered, returning the princess' smile. "I am utterly devoted to you."

Relief seemed to wash over the noble lady then and her eyes watered too, "Oh Mirella, thank you." She flung her thin arms around her older maid, hugging her in such an unprecedented display of affection. "There's so much I need to tell you now."

"I'm all yours, Princess. Just tell me how I can help you! What of your Prince?" Mirella prodded, seeming so sincere as she moved towards the other woman, her voice so low.

With a sweetly devious smile the fair princess welcomed the close, conspiratorial turn. "I've been in touch with him all along," she whispered. "And now the time has come where we can do more than just wait, Mirella." Her eyes dipped to her servant's pregnant stomach, and darted away immediately. She obviously didn't care to linger on that thought or more precisely the guilt from it.

"How?" Mirella gasped, honestly taken away that the girl had any bit of cleverness to her at all. She had not been expecting the woman to have a plan, let alone having found a means to contact him.

Looking so smugly confident she pursed her lips and looked for a while as if she'd not say a word. "Remember the locket the prince gave me at our betrothal ceremony?" she asked, fishing into her lacy, frilled dress and pulling out the exquisitely crafted silver filigree locket. "I can speak to him at night with this," she whispered. Her blue eyes were so wide with excitement, "But what's most important is that..." she took a moment to calm herself. "He's told me he's marching here right now. And will arrive within a week to free us all."

"That's fantastic news," she gasped, Mirella's exotically shaped eyes widening. "Princess, you are too clever! How many does he have? What should I do?"

Her servant's excitement only seemed to stoke her own, but she held up her pale, delicate hands in a gesture to quiet them both. "We have to be calm. We can't show our true feelings, Mirella," she cautioned. "If that blackheart finds out it could spoil things and cause the prince more time and lives than need be," she said with a bit of that haughty air of a ruler.

Mirella nodded, bowing her head, "Of course, my princess. I will keep myself contained, in service of you always."

Princess Anabelle smiled confidently and touched Mirella's hand. "I need you to get a message to the people, Mirella. But you must be circumspect," she cautioned. "There is a resistance in the city, I know it," she stated with absolutely certainty. "So you must get word to them to be prepared. If they get word beforehand they can ignite the city into open rebellion so that those heathen dogs will be caught between both forces and utterly annihilated." There was a certain malicious gleam in her eyes then, one Mirella knew well.

"I will do all I can, Princess. I know there are those that would eagerly rebel," she nodded eagerly.

"Tell me, how many can we count on to join our fight?"

With a shrug of her slender shoulders she said, "I don't know, to be honest. Though I'm hoping it's all of them." She gave a hopeful smile. "I know they are out there though. The prince had contact with them up until recently, but he can't get word in anymore." She squeezed Mirella's hand, "It's up to you to find them and help save my people."

"It is my privilege and duty, Princess. You expect him in a week, that gives us plenty of time to plan a coordinated attack," she mused to herself, but all the while the wheels in her head were turning. "Why can he no longer rally them?"

She shrugged her shoulders and looked down, "Something about that blackheart barbarian closing off the city from their old lines of communication," she said. The princess was never one for details. She was accustomed to giving broad orders and expecting them to be obeyed, leaving the details to those who'd carry them out.

Mirella shook her head, but then smiled, "Then I will pick up where he left off." She looked so honest, so trustworthy, but for that moment she hated the princess like she never had before. "Is there anything else you need?"

The smiling princess reached into a pocket and pulled out one of the royal seals. "Show this to the rebels in case they need convincing of who you are. This is the most important moment of your life, Mirella," she said with such certainty, the noble willing to mark the value of another's life at the drop of a hat. "When this is done, you shall be handmaiden to the princess who helped save beautiful Ariste from the barbarian hordes," she said with a proud smile.

She accepted the token with such a display of reverence, secreting it away against her swollen bosom, "I am so grateful that you trusted me, Princess. You will not be disappointed."

With a bright smile she gestured towards the large platter of food, "You can secret out as much food as you like, Mirella. I'm told the people are starving on the streets and," her eyes flickered down again, "even if it is the spawn of a rapist barbarian... you are with child now, and need to take care of yourself." There was almost even sympathy in those words.

Mirella hadn't thought about the plight of the people in so long, she was surprised to hear her say that, though she quickly covered it up with a look of appreciation. "Thank you, Princess," she said as she went to gather some food, ever obedient and willing to please.

Anabelle led her to the door after she secreted some of the rich delights into her ratty old robes. "You're dismissed," she said in her normal, haughty tone. "Perhaps we shall speak again soon." The guard outside opened the door and paid not a glance to the two women as she let Mirella out.

Free of the incessant blather of Anabelle, her footsteps became sure and angry, her face flushed with rage. That little bitch.

"I need to speak with the God-King," she said sternly, "Where can I find him?"

# CHAPTER 11

At the top of the roadway that led to the palace stood her ruler and master. Towering above all others, a northerner in elaborate dress—though all hides and horns—knelt before him. "We were wrong ta doubt the true God-King," he declared in subservience before her lover Kulav. "My men are now yours. And we thank ya for yer generosity in allowin' us this opportunity to join with your ranks after refusing our share of the glory in conquest."

It was a solemn occasion she realized; a Chieftain of one of the northern tribes of Ka'reem was swearing himself to the God-King.

"Arise," came his command in that husky, masculine voice. "You are welcomed into the ranks, and I promise there shall be more glory to come." The chieftain, a massive man in his own right though not so tall as her lord and lover, backed away and said not a word more, looking too fearful to dare such a thing.

As that little display ended the warlord turned and saw her there watching.

"Your Greatness," her head tilted downwards as she strode towards him. "The princess has been scheming." She paused, licking over her lips. She was once more in her casual garb, the slutty little outfit showing off her advanced pregnancy, and there was no shame in her motions at all. She was proud to give him a child, and to show off how her body contorted because of him.

Hearing the tidings of her news he placed his hand on her shoulder and guided her away from the open spot. Taking her off to the side in one of the nooks along the palace walls he bent his head and spoke with her in a private tone. "Tell me everything," he commanded

Her voice was so soft as she looked up at her God, "The Prince will be arriving inside of a week. The Princess has been using a trinket to speak with him, and he has been communicating with rebels inside of the city. Something you have done a week ago has interrupted his communication with them and she wishes for me to rally them," she said so quickly. "She has given me a token to convince them I am on her side, and is unaware of the numbers the Prince has with him. She is confident it is enough."

As stoic as ever she could not read the ashen giant, his beautifully masculine face passive as he pondered her information. "Describe everything in detail," he ordered, and after hearing of the entire encounter in its minutiae he squeezed her shoulder. "You did well. Very well," he said approvingly. "With any luck you've bought us enough time to act and put a stop to this," he declared. Through his hard look she saw it there: a faint glimmer of approval and thanks that far eclipsed anything the princess had ever given her in all her years of service.

He made her at once feel weak and strong, and her mouth parted just so. "I wasn't aware the Princess could scheme at all, so I imagine it has been the Prince telling her what to do. When we kill him, she will crumble." She wanted him so badly, then. It was more than devotion, more than love. It was a hunger that she had no control over, and her small, private smile was filled with affection.

That made the dark man smile, and he brought his hand up to her cheek, cupping it and stroking his thumb across her smooth face as he stood before her in his usual garb, his bare chest on display. "I hope you are right. When I return from the campaign to wipe out the prince's army, we shall find out," he said solemnly.

"Do nothing to alert the princess to your true devotions," he cautioned. "I ride out in the morning," he declared to her, the calculating warlord having already taken time to decide his actions. "While I'm away I am inducting you into the order of my concubine-warriors." He turned abruptly and began to storm off, leaving her with no choice but to follow.

As he passed the concubines tent he called out to Svella, the woman looking ready to give birth any day now. "You shall handle Mirella's induction into your order. Heed her warnings." He cautioned, never ceasing his movement into the palace as the tall warrior woman looked to Mirella with a stunning lack of surprise.

"Welcome then, sister," she intoned with a light respect, her lips forming into an almost amused smile.

Mirella liked the woman and nodded her head, "I hope the others take this with a similar mood," she grinned. "This day is turning out less than I imagined."

With a laugh Svella, topless and as shameless in her nudity as Mirella had become, guided her to the tent. "You shall conquer all, for the spirit of the God-King is with you," she declared, leading her in to spread the news to the others.

# CHAPTER 12

Her induction into the warrior-concubines was less ceremonious and more business than she would've expected. The entire palace complex was in an uproar as everyone rushed about, preparing to muster out for war.

It wasn't until the middle of the night that she was taken back in to see him, and he was still conducting business, pointing out things to his chieftain-generals on a great hide map. "Be prepared, for at sunset we ride. This little princeling shall not catch us unawares in this city. We shall crush him on the fields as is our way," he demanded. The sweaty, hairy northerners slammed their fists to their chests repeatedly and let loose a roar that echoed throughout the halls before retreating, leaving him to ponder over the map alone.

It gave her time to study him in private, his cloak hung over his back in such a way that she could see almost his entire chest. Those hard muscles so firmly outlined, such a vision of male perfection that gleamed in the lantern light of the palace.

She loved staring at him. She still often went to the crude statue when he was busy, her eyes working over the stone and filling in the gaps where the sculptor had failed. She lusted for him in a way she never had for anyone before, and found his masculine appeal to be sweet perfection. She didn't fear for him, nor doubt for a second that he would kill the Prince, yet she dreaded being without him for the length of time it would take.

Mirella knew, however, he would be counting on her, and as her bare feet moved over the smooth marble floor, she looked confident. "Your Greatness," she announced herself.

He wasn't disturbed by her, though she couldn't imagine how he might've predicted her approach, as silent as it was. "Come here," said that god of a man in his dark voice. "Tomorrow I ride off into the greatest battle of my life," he stated, putting his arm around her. His eyes remained glued to the hide map. The guesses as to the size of the imperial army were so wildly different, but even the most conservative put it at well over what they could potentially field; double at least.

"And soon you will ride home after the greatest victory," she promised, her body pressing against his side as her arm wrapped around his back. She was short compared to him, with beautiful olive skin and long, glossy black hair, and the pregnancy did little to interfere with her looks. She was not youthful, but in his presence, she was vibrant.

His strong hand stroked over her back and side, the coarse feel of his hard grasp so comforting. It was the touch of someone who knew hard labour. He was a ruler because he had made it so, not because he was born into it like the princess.

She caught his gaze then, he looked to her, finally diverting his attention from the map. "While I am away I am putting my concubine-warriors in charge of running the city," he explained. "They will not ride to war with me, but remain here. They are the only ones I can trust fully to do this. And you shall help them. If, as you say, the princess knows of some rebels, then they shall rise up with or without warning once they know my forces are out of the city."

His hand gripped her backside, squeezing her round ass and pushed her in against his hard body. "You could be integral in helping them maintain order here."

"I won't fail you," she promised. She was deadly serious, for there was no way she would allow the city to fall, for him to ride back victorious only to have to clean up after their failure. "If there's anything you need, please, Your Greatness. I am always at your service."

His strong, guiding hand brought her to the table. He very forcibly brought her up onto it to sit upon the edge, squeezing her full, fleshy thigh as he stared into her gaze. "I will not sleep this night," he said to her, "but I need comfort and satisfaction before I ride out."

Those dark features of his were stunning in the glowing light of the lanterns; it almost seemed as if the darkness helped irradiate his ashen skin. So as he leaned in and tilted his head to kiss her, she saw such a vision of male beauty, then felt his hungry, needful, doting lips meet hers, smacking noisily in the large hall.

Her passion was only met by his, and her soft tongue probed his mouth. Hands wrapped around his shoulders, squeezing his flesh so tightly as a moan erupted between them. She needed him. Loved him. Worshiped him.

Tomorrow she'd fight for him, but today, she'd give him what he needed with such desire that he'd never dare die.

At some point during their night of passion they had moved into the bedroom again, so she awoke upon his bed in time to hear the sound of hooves, weapons and armour in the courtyard below. It was such a clattering cacophony of noise that only an army could've made such a noise to reach that far up.

Mirella was sore and weary still. He had been bestial and insatiable, taking her the whole night through, doing such things to her that her mind would buzz with the memories for months more to come.

Yet still she bounded from the bed—as much as a pregnant, properly fucked woman could bound—and stared at the scene below. Her heart raced as she grabbed up her new clothing, moving through the castle at such a speed.

She emerged onto such a sight. There they were, hundreds of the mounted northerners—the Ka'reem—filing out on horseback through the palace gates to the roadway that led through the mountains. They looked, individually, like such hairy savages, but as a group in full war gear, they looked fearsome and mighty.

But most significant of all, there he was. Her beloved ruler.

He sat upon the back of a great horse, blacker than he, its coat glistened in the morning light. Its legs so thick and sturdy, hooves wide and large, and all about armour was strapped to the beast's sides.

Atop it sat the God-King Kulav in full battle regalia. It looked much like his usual clothes, the high boots and cloak much the same. But they were armoured now. His chest was garbed in a chain mail vest that showed but glimpses of his dark flesh beneath. About his shoulders the plumes of raven's feathers and on his head a half-helm that made him look like some terrifying demon-bird from out of folktales.

He oversaw the orderly procession of the troops, fully absorbed in the affair as he gave orders to his subordinates.

She watched in such awe, such appreciation for all he'd done. Knowing his past, how far he'd risen; it was only more impressive than when she'd first met him, striding into the room and knocking his own warriors aside.

When finally he began to pull his horse forward

to join the procession he caught sight of her, and she saw the glint of his dark eyes from beneath his helm. He was terrifying and majestic atop his warhorse, an inspiration to his warriors and doubtless a horror to his enemies. And she caught his gaze, held it.

He didn't wave or call out or in any way draw attention to it in any matter except to watch her, keep her gaze. That was special enough, for she was the last he saw before his horse trotted out of the courtyard and onto the road to war.

She waited for some time and finally it was Svella who came to greet her. "If only we could ride with him again to war," she said with some sadness to her voice.

"We have an important task," she said, though there was a lingering sorrow in her tone as well, edged with hard determination. "We have to keep what is His so that when He returns, victorious, He may rest."

The tall northern woman looked to her with an appreciative stare then nodded. "It is as you say," she remarked. "Now come sister. If we are to administer justice then we need our war raiments too."

She led Mirella to a special place where the warrior-concubines kept their supplies. There she found uniforms like the raven-garbed elite who marched in with the Seer—Kulav's mother—and an array of weapons, curved scimitars, shields, daggers, and many bows.

It didn't matter than she barely knew how to fight, but for a few training sessions back in her homeland to the south. She so rarely thought of them, though, yet as she reached for a scimitar, it felt right. She spared no time getting dressed and resumed practice against the air, getting used to the weight and the speed of the blade.

Svella watched her with some curiosity, "You are not trained as we are," she put it delicately. "But I can correct that in ti—" it was then they were interrupted by one of the other loyal concubines, her raven helm pulled up as she spoke breathlessly.

"The Seer!" she cried. "She has fallen into a trance," and the look of anxiousness on her face told them both this was urgent.

Svella put down the weapon she held and took the scimitar from Mirella. "Come, we must go to her."

Mirella didn't even waste time at being offended, instead following after the woman in her heavier armour, finding it uncomfortably restrictive after wearing almost nothing for so many months. She didn't allow herself to feel dread or panic, instead forcing calm to the surface.

The chamber that had been taken over for the Seer was formerly a chapel of worship for the noble family. Now the great chamber was adorned in the holy symbols and markings of the superstitious Ka'reem, the markings of the God-King all about: the sign of the raven.

At the head of the room where once the pulpit stood was now the great raised bed of Kulav's mother. The pale white woman twitched and spasmed, shivering in some unknown misery as she stared off into the ceiling.

Mirella had found the old woman as frustrating

as she was fascinating, but the crone frightened her. The truth, the knowledge, and how easily she saw through her was terrifying, even though she had nothing to hide from the woman. The respect she felt for the Mother of a God was eternal, and her reverence ran hand in hand with the jumble of emotions.

The other women were deathly silent, watching in awe and fear as the Seer shook and spasmed. It was terrifying to see, though not only because of the power the woman held, but because Mirella—alone amongst the women—knew something of the suffering she had endured and must now still be enduring.

After watching long in silence Svella whispered to her. "The last time this happened she was said not to come out of it for days."

"We don't have days," Mirella murmured, already uneasy about leaving the city proper. She feared that at any moment, the abused and wretched would begin their revolt, and when she turned her face back to the woman, she silently prayed for her to find peace enough to speak.

With a shake of her head Svella added, "But when she came out of her trance... she bestowed upon the God-King the warning that won him the war against Ariste. It is said she is the line to the spirits that lets our Lord and Master reign with the power of a deity."

The bridge of her nose crinkled in distaste, but she said no more on it. Still, as her arms folded across her stomach and she felt that mass move within her, she hoped it wasn't too late. For him. For them. "We need to prepare for the rebels," she said softly.

# CHAPTER 13

The warrior-concubines set up their command from within the Seer's chamber. The women charged with her care and security refused to leave her be, and all understood the importance of getting whatever news she had immediately.

Though days of planning and action turned up little. Svella shook her head as she came in with her full armour on, acting untroubled by the pregnant belly that looked well past its time. "The latest searches have turned up nothing," she said.

"This doesn't seem right," Mirella frowned, finding herself restless and her nerves frayed in a way they'd never been before. It was torture not knowing, being uncertain of what was happening in the battle, of the status of their troops. She was looking forward to fighting the rebels if only for something to do, to take her mind off of her anxiety.

Mirella had gone out personally with Svella, the soldier-sisters patrolling the streets. She had seen the terrible state of the city, the invasion and isolation of Ariste having had drastic consequences for the population. But through it they'd turned up nothing as yet.

Svella opened her mouth to talk but then her eyes went wide as she stared beyond the shorter Mirella.

That look of awe could mean only one thing, and as Mirella turned and looked she saw the Seer sat up on her bed, peacefully still. She was no longer the quivering mass entrapped in some violent seizure, she looked serene and beautiful. She looked every bit fit to play the part of the mother of a god.

She felt like she could weep, and was surprised at how much of it was simple joy that the woman suffered no longer. At least for the moment. A lump was in her throat and she moved forward to the woman, brazen as always. Even surrounded by the elite guard, by those that cared for the woman and held her in such esteem, there was no holding Mirella back.

A gasp travelled through the other women and she saw as one went to take hold of her and keep her from approaching the Seer. Instead the ghostly woman stirred in her flowing blood-red robes and her eyes fluttered open to look directly at Mirella. "My son marches to victory... marches to death!" The way her voice went from serene to shrilly-panicked in no time was chilling.

She felt her eyes burn but still she approached the Seer, kneeling at the foot of the bed. She paid no heed to those behind her, instead raising her eyes to the Mother of her God. She felt that horrible, dry lump in her throat as she shook her head childishly, but still she dared not speak. Dared not yet interrupt the woman's lucidity.

She watched as the pale woman's eyes rolled back into her head then fought it off, as if struggling to retain control. "He shall find victory on the battlefield... but the enemy comes to steal his prize from beneath his nose even now. If they are not stopped..." she clutched the sides of her head and rocked back and forth, the whole of the room seeming to change. She felt a shifting in the air, the candles flickering all about though nothing seemed to have changed.

"The princess," she hissed, pushing herself to stand. "Svella," she moved to the other woman the brushed past, "Let me know of anything else she says. I need some that can actually fight." Bitter resentment flourished up within her, betrayal struck in her heart. "That little bitch will pay."

"No!" shrieked the Seer, her piercing scream blood curdling. "It is too late!"

She stared at Mirella, and that gaze chilled her, as if something inhuman was inside the pale woman. "An army marches through secret tunnels in the mountains right now! No force of arms can stop them!" she cried.

The other women seemed to get it, they all rose standing and froze in some look of solemn resignation.

Mirella froze, her breathing stilled as she turned back to the crone. "You can't expect for us to sit and wait for our deaths, Mother," she said softly. Her footsteps were slow as she approached the woman, and once more she knelt, her eyes holding such reverence. "We carry your grandchildren. Your blood. You said as much yourself. That I could be a Witch of the Coven."

The other women crowded around the bed and Svella gave Mirella a sympathetic look, she murmured, "It is not as you think, sister." She heard the scuffle of booted feet as another woman hurried out of the room and then the remaining women began to link hands about the bed. She heard chanting begin as the white haired woman swayed.

Mirella was lost, but she wouldn't let him down. She couldn't. Her eyes blinked away the tears once more as she stared up at the Seer, "I would do anything for him," she said earnestly. "My life is nothing compared to his. He deserves this city to fall to their knees." She looked up and around at the swaying women. "What's not as I think? Have you all given up?"

The doors swung open again and she saw as more of the Raven Guard women scurried in. All about the chambers they began to join hands and the chanting grew louder. Svella took Mirella's hand and squeezed it tightly, "Join in, sister," she urged and began to chant with the rest.

Her hand was trembling as she joined with them, welcomed into the folds of women so unlike herself, but as the tears began to stream down her cheeks, there was so little else she could do. At least this felt like something. Like nothing. A sweet distraction at the precipice of destruction and failure.

Her failure.

It was then she heard it, the old woman's voice in her mind. "Do not despair," it said, sounding so much younger and stronger than it really was. "We do not resign ourselves to giving up on him... we resign ourselves to sacrifice for him," she told her, though looking at the old woman she had not moved from her swaying. Did not speak out loud.

Mirella blinked. Her heart quickened, and immediately she knew she would not feel sad for this thing. For this sacrifice, and only the loss of her child—his child—resonated within her. She'd always known, from the first moment she saw him, that she would do anything for him.

He'd done more for her in the short months than she'd dreamed of in those tentative, uncertain moments of just meeting him. In the days of new lust and love and appreciation. In the warm nights of comfort in his bed, he'd always brought her to new heights of devotion.

The old woman's voice spoke to her in such a soothing, youthful tone, "You are willing to give all. Your dedication is admirable. I could not have chosen a better woman for my son," she complimented, the chanting becoming a hum on the air that seemed to vibrate reality itself, everything beginning to turn bizarrely blurry about her.

"Your child shall not be harmed," said the Seer to

her again in her mind. "And you shall survive this to sacrifice another day. Now I impart to you the secrets you need for that..."

It was then Mirella felt it. The earth shattering truth of the Ka'reem women and their powers. She felt it. Their coven commanded the ability to rip the earth asunder if they wished it. They could destroy as well as create, but she saw it... flashes of sacrifice. The Seer's madness a price she paid for her son. She saw then other women who paid various other fees for their power. All terrifying. Their bodies shrivelled to husks. Some left hideous and deformed. All suffered regrets no matter how hard they tried to deny it, for the price was never easy to pay.

She wasn't aware that the tears kept streaming, that she could feel something so strongly, so passionately and with such empathy as she did then. Years of being a servant, of growing up as a dredge of society had left her with a hardened shell. She cared not for the suffering of others, not after seeing how jaded they were about her own pain. It was something practical and cruel that kept her sane, but for that moment she knew the exquisite despair of so many others and she could empathize. She knew that she too would make this sacrifice and become someone different.

Someone he potentially would no longer love.

She acknowledged the regrets she'd have, and still knew she'd do it. Sacrifice all she valued, even His love, in order to save His kingdom.

Mirella had offered up all she could, and the chanting took on such a powerful force. When finally she felt the shuddering of the room coalesce it was as if all the women were one. Their unified purpose causing them to see into powers beyond.

The Seer guided them, she knew that innately, their sight travelling through the stone of the palace and into the mountains themselves upon which it was built. She saw then in the tunnels, the soldiers travelling ancient hewn paths the nobles and miners before them had made. Their numbers seemed endless and beyond the mining paths the soldiers in such numbers were marching through great halls hewn by beings that could not have been human judging by their choice of style.

There had to be hundreds, at least a thousand, of them. All heavily armoured and bent on coming to Ariste and taking the city that Kulav had won.

Together the witches—for she was one of them now—put their will to it. The walls of the cave began to shake, pebbles slipped from the stonework above. The soldiers did not notice it at first, but as they did she saw the looks of panic on their faces.

An earthquake, they cried. She didn't hear it as such, but sensed it. Terror took hold of them and as rubble began to fall in their midst striking some, knocking them wounded or unconscious, the rest began to scurry as they could. They trampled one another, losing their military discipline as the stonework began to crumble.

The rest was bloody horror.

The women had ripped an army to pieces with their minds and as they came out of the spell they knew they had felt victory. Though the price...

Several of the women collapsed, others went to them. Some cried out in warbling pain or madness. Mirella however...

Nothing had changed. She felt it. She was as before. She was free to see things all as they were: the Seer collapsed, the anguish on her sister's faces. Then felt the rumbling that should've ceased. That had killed so many soldiers and now shook the palace itself.

She didn't quite feel panic, not as she felt she should. There was newfound concern and affection for the women, brought about by the shared experience, but it wasn't panic. Her eyes moved over them, over her God's Mother, over her sisters and the price they paid.

What was her price?

Her hands went to her stomach, to her womb, and felt for a stir, for that familiar life within her, even as she felt the ground tremble beneath her. "We need to get into the open air," she said, though she had no idea if she had whispered it or screamed it.

She felt the same, yet the shock had made her mind fuzzy.

Things all happened so fast from there it seemed, as if it was all a haze. She felt the reassuring life within her stir, knew it was well, and all about Svella and her gathered the women that were still able and got them to bring the others to safety.

It was barely a moment too soon, for one of the stonework statues toppled, crushing the bed upon which the Seer formerly lay as the quaking continued. Then out into the courtyard they still felt it. More than that they heard the mountains themselves groan and quake. It was such a terrifying sound.

It was as if the world itself was crying out in agony at their act of violence and then... she saw it even from where she was. All the other women gawked around her. The mountain began to crumble, great slabs of stone sheering off the side of the collapsing rock cliffs. Falling down into the pass out of which the God King had rode but days before.

Rushing to the parapets Svella and her stood on shaky legs as the quaking finally slowed and came to a stop. He may have ridden through that passage to war, but he would not ride back along it. It was closed. And no force she could imagine—short of the terrifying powers they just wielded—could dislodge such debris again.

# CHAPTER 14

The quakes had finally stopped. Svella and Mirella had rallied the sisters to reassert control over the situation. The city was in a panic after all. Nobody knew what had just happened, talk of dark signs were on everyone's lips.

Svella slumped down in a chair at their new headquarters, cradling her pregnant belly. She was well overdue now, and looked enormous, weary.

Mirella, meanwhile, had been doting, caring on the other women. On her sister's. She wasn't much use in battle, but she excelled at tending to others, and for the only time in her life aside from her God, she wanted to help them.

"You're past your date," Mirella tsked as her hand ran through Svella's hair.

With a snort the tall woman retorted, "What gave

it away?" She gently patted the giant stomach she sported. "The God-King has blessed me with a mighty child, sister. This one takes time," she intoned, sounding amused. Talk of him only reminded her of the ugly truth. The mountain was closed. Even if he won... what then? He couldn't get back.

She'd long ago figured this was the cost. Her cost.

"He will be proud," she said. She wouldn't entirely give up hope. After all, even if he didn't return to this kingdom, he would rule others. Take on other concubines, raise other armies, and she wouldn't allow herself to feel self-pity.

Svella had never spoken of her price. None of the women did. Even those whose price was obvious—so blatantly obvious—was respectfully ignored by the others. It was not talked about. Ever.

It was shared yet personal, or perhaps it was because talking of it led to comparisons. One woman talking of her great sacrifice as more than another's. Whatever the reason they did not discuss such things, and they thought it best that way.

"He will be," echoed the taller woman, stroking her stomach. They were all concerned for him, Mirella realized. Even those who feared him more than loved him. Nobody even much worried that the mountain pass cut them off from the bulk of the cities already dwindled food supply in the farms on the other side of the mountain.

"What of the princess?" asked Svella. "How has she reacted to this whole... thing?" she didn't want to say more on the incident itself. The witches didn't care for talking about it.

"The Princess handles bad news poorly. I haven't wished to see her."

It was left unspoken. Mirella was worried that she couldn't pretend. Her emotions were rubbed raw, and the way her fingertips braided Svella's hair a bit faster was the only demonstration of her agitation.

"Maybe it will have shaken her. Get her to tell more," she suggested, the two women having grown so close in the intervening period. There was no jealously guarded idea with Svella; she wished only to help her fellow sisters. Mirella especially.

"Perhaps you're right," she agreed, finishing the braid and lovingly putting it over the woman's shoulder, stroking her flesh. "How is the Seer?"

The tall northern woman sighed, "She has not awoken since. She pays a tremendous price for us all," she intoned with some glumness. Mirella wasn't the only one to feel for the Mother's plight.

Her lips touched the woman's head before she pulled away, "I will see to the Princess, though I feel that if you give birth here and now it may be less painful," she teased. It was a dark sense of humour, one that she had never known herself to have until now.

Svella gave a deep laugh, and though she normally would've accompanied her, the pregnancy—and their ever increasing duties—were keeping her weary and she stayed resting in her chair. "Good luck with the harpy queen."

Since the quaking Mirella was seen by the other soldiers and workers more and more as something of a leader. They paid her deference as she passed through the halls towards the Princess's room, even gave her occasional salutes and bows.

Entering into that decadent chamber however, she found the princess looking anxious. Her beautiful, luxurious blonde hair a bit frazzled. "Mirella!" she cried, dressed in some gorgeous sky-blue gown with frilled edges.

She hated her for that decadence, for that pampered look even in her despair, but her face softened as she hugged the princess and the first tear slipped from her eye without permission. She missed him. She couldn't show her weakness in front of the other women, even in front of her friend, but in private, in the arms of this woman she loathed, she brushed that wayward tear away.

"Princess, I'm so happy you're safe."

The princess was not concerned for her distress however. "What has happened, Mirella?!" She cried. "The shaking... the mountain!" she cried, pointing out her balcony to the collapsed mountain path. "What madness is this?! What's happened?!"

"I don't know, Princess. We had begun to rally when I first heard word of the marching of the troops, so much closer than expected. And then..." she trailed off. She had no way of answering the woman, and another tear slipped past her cheek, even as her green eyes remained focused. "We are frightened and lost. Have you heard from the Prince? From anyone on the outside?"

The princess began to pace, clutching the sides of her head with her long nailed fingers. "You found them then?" She looked so distressed. "The last I heard from the prince, he... he said the loyal citizens were hidden out in the old aqueduct." She stopped and looked to her, "Are those the ones you found? Are they okay? Did the quake hurt them?!" She demanded her answers so insistently, looking near panic.

Mirella blinked away more tears, trying to win control over her body as she shook her head, "We don't know, Princess." Her words struck her, her tongue lacing over her mouth as she thought it over. "When did you find this out?"

The princess began to wring her hands nervously, resuming her pacing. "What do you mean you don't know?" she said. "We have to find out! Didn't you come from there?" she looked so lost and confused, her worries tearing her apart.

"The dust is still settling, Princess, and I needed more help. I couldn't do it on my own," she said softly, looking positively brow beaten. Maybe she was. She'd felt like she lost a bit of herself since the cave in. "We will find them."

That mollified the dainty young woman and she nodded as she paced. "Good. Good!" She said, gnawing her lower lip with concern. "The prince will be delayed a bit," she said. "With the mountain pass collapsed he'll... he'll," she rubbed her forehead. "He'll have to clear it or go around the Arisean Mountains. Which... which might take months," she muttered, sounding distraught.

"Princess, I ever continue to work for your good name," she said, but her voice was so soft.

The princess nodded, "Good, Mirella. You go, you go and... do what you can," she said. "I'll..." she paused, "wait!"

She rushed to her ornate desk and sat down, writing out in her beautiful, ornate script a letter, then using wax to close it with the royal seal. She went to Mirella, "Here. Take this to my loyal subjects," she said. "This should buoy their spirits," she decreed confidently.

Mirella clutched it and nodded, looking at the young, frantic woman. Even in the throes of despair, she was vibrant. Vivacious. Mirella bowed her head respectfully, "I won't let you down."

The exchange ended there, the princess too caught up in her own worries to offer more encouragement. So once Mirella had left her and got outside she read the letter. It contained a rather drawn out spiel about nothing in particular, but at the end she saw something. The princess made mention of a lord she referred to as "wise".

Mirella had known the young princess since she was a little girl, and the only person she had ever thought was wise was the sleazy old priest that managed to bilk both nobles and commoners out of their fortunes. The same one who once led services in the royal family's chapel.

She folded it back up, and for a few moments, she found a private room and let herself feel that all-consuming pain she'd been avoiding since the cave-in. It was disappointment in herself, in her failure and her inactivity. It was terror for her lover. It was a resentment that she hadn't given birth yet, and at her body's inability to fight.

But when she got it all out, when she felt all that pain flood from her body, she felt refreshed and rejuvenated. She would find them. An aqueduct that could be her salvation.

# CHAPTER 15

As Mirella approached the Raven Guard's headquarters where her other sisters received their orders, she heard the noise of heavy breathing. Rushing inside she saw Svella there alone, panting and looking strained as her knees were spread. She grimaced and looked to her, "Sister... it is time," she groaned.

"Finally," Mirella intoned, placing the letter aside as she moved to her friend. "This is a sign of things to come, Svella. You will give birth to a child of God, and we will bring Him home," she stated, her confidence returned. She'd never delivered a child, but she'd helped once or twice when others were desperate, and she quickly began barking orders.

The rush of activity that came as the other woman obeyed her, gathering what was needed.

Mirella may not have done this before, but the other women of the Guard certainly had. It was something they'd shared for some time now, and she needed only stand back and watch as they rushed to do what needed done.

# CHAPTER 16

When finally Svella cradled her new son she was more exhausted then Mirella had ever seen her. The pregnancy was long, going on for hours on end, and she'd lost a lot of blood. But the large boy, so dark, so much like his father, seemed to please the mother greatly. "He will be proud," she stated to Mirella again with confidence on her uncharacteristically weak voice, a smile on her lips as the other women watched enviously.

Mirella, however, was only pleased for her friend. She had feared that she'd feel that jealousy, that deep feeling of loathing, but instead she was only grateful that mother and child made it through, safe.

"I will see to it that He's home to see him soon," Mirella said softly, pressing her lips to Svella's forehead. "Rest. I have to find a wise man."

Svella was too weary to question that, instead she just gave a wry laugh as if her friend were up to some shenanigans again. The other women however, took her seriously and they rushed to her call.

It wasn't long before they had formed up behind her as their troops, and they marched into the streets. The Ka'reem warriors typically rode on horseback at all times, but in the city and on such a mission as this they went by foot instead.

She led them through the damaged streets of Ariste, its beautiful white stonework chipped, damaged or otherwise burnt by the invasion and the quakes. Its people were hiding, for though the main force of the occupation army was gone, they still feared the tall Amazonian warriors in their terrifying black raiment.

Mirella didn't have to search long. For though the largest, richest homes had been confiscated for the Ka'reem occupiers, the commoners still had their church. She heard their prayers even from outside, and as they pushed in she saw him. Priest Quaylin, fat off the wealth of others as he preached from the pulpit.

Her eyes were hard, that green gaze falling on the slob of a man. She wondered how much he was getting, or thought he'd be getting, for saving the poor Princess. Her arms folded across her chest, across the raven feathered garb as she scanned the crowd, listening to his sermon.

The hall was rich, for though it allowed commoners Ariste was a beautiful city regardless, and would not suffer worshippers to go into a less than beautiful space. From out of the spiralling columns she heard the echo of the priests voice travel down to her. "The gods shall gift to us freedom, my children! Hold true to your faith and the line of rightfully appointed rulers, and you shall be delivered unto the bliss you once had and deserve."

The dozens who were there were listening attentively, and she noticed amongst them some former nobles, now dressed in more raggedy clothing as they were forced to live like commoners. "A test from above!" cried the priest. "Our faith in their will has waned, and so they've taken their holy children from us by the unleashing of these dogs from the north! Show your true loyalty to the gods, restore your true rulers and they shall reward your faithfulness."

She didn't feel pity for the formerly privileged, who had slung insults and ignored her as something less than human. Like a dog. Like the northerners. She was nothing to them in the great halls, and in the beautiful church, they were nothing to her.

Nothing but heretics to her God.

"Priest Quaylin," she said as she entered the hall. "I need to speak with you."

Silence took over the chapel, silence but for the echoing boot steps of over a dozen armed Raven Guard marching down the leviathan halls of the chapel. The priest went wide-eyed and slack-jawed, his bald head sinking down. "T-traitor," he managed out, though the word barely managed to carry through the room, despite his earlier bombasticity.

It was true. She stood out as a traitor amidst the

Raven Guard. They were all statuesque pale women, she was short, darker skinned.

"You've betrayed your own people for wealth and fortune. Surely I'm just following in your footsteps, oh wise one," she hissed bitterly.

Her devoted sisters marched quickly, passing her, flanking her side and keeping the parishioners at bay as she strode towards the altar.

The priest backed away, and looked towards the rear doors. "Rise up, my fellow Aristeans! Spread the word! Your true leaders shall be restored and you shall be rewarded!" The hall was struck dumb and silent though, they watched, weak and hungry in disbelief as this last sacred ground was violated.

She turned her back on the priest, instead looking towards the supplicants. "There is no help. This is life, and you are not comfortable with it. I appreciate that. You may not remember me, but I know toil. I know torment, and for more than thirty years, I've served. I've scrounged. I've gone to bed hungry and sore, stained from the day and with the knowledge that it will only happen again the next. And the day after."

Mirella's voice gained confidence and power as she spoke to the former nobles and commoners, "I still serve. I still work hard, tirelessly, for my betters. The difference is that now, my betters deserve their place. They've fought for it, and won it. They've known the pleasure and pain of hard work, of dedication. Of power hard won and harder kept. This man knows only greed. Envy. He wishes he were born like you, into a home of wealth and tidings, and instead he is forced to take from others. To lie to them. Manipulate them."

She turned back towards the priest, her emerald eyes turned stony, "God does not care for thieves."

The people were stunned by her outburst, and as she lectured them the priest turned and ran for the back door, screaming as he left. "Rise up!" he cried, though the people in the chapel instead screamed and panicked themselves. They tried to run around the pews and take off into the streets. There were so many of them the Raven Guard couldn't hope to contain them entirely, instead they focussed on containing those they could.

"Useless Aristeans," Mirella muttered, looking around idly at the tidings of the old religion, and she wondered briefly if the Princess would hear of this. She fingered the letter as she began to walk out the back door, following after the priest as she took in the panic around her.

The door led to a hallway that went down into the basement, and two of her Guard sisters joined her. "We'll apprehend him, sister," they said with respect, taking off down the stairs after the portly old man. Those were fit guardswomen, not showing signs of pregnancy, and she had no doubt they would catch up to him before long.

She trusted them. It was a new feeling, for even in her life before, she'd never trusted the other servants. Even those she called her friends, she understood that they would take from her if they needed it badly enough, yet these women that were so sceptical at first had become something stronger.

As she moved back into the church, she settled into one of the benches, her eyes going up along the beautiful architecture, and for a brief spell, she felt at peace.

She felt closer to her God—the God-King—and before she even realized she was doing it, she had spoken a modified prayer, bidding his safe return. It had only taken a moment, but it felt good.

# CHAPTER 17

They hadn't even gotten the priest back to the palace when chaos began to break loose in the city below. The fleeing former-nobles spread word of the desecration of the altar and the apprehension of the priest and the lower classes—already hungry and desperate—were pushed to their limits.

At the top of the hill Mirella had looked back and saw the swarms of people move through Ariste's winding roads, torches and whatever implements to use as makeshift weapons that they could find.

Arriving into the tent that formerly housed the God-King's concubines but was now the concubine-warriors headquarters, the other women were buzzing about getting ready. They were small in number compared to the masses of revolting citizens below, but they were highly trained and battle hardened.

One of the younger members of their order came up to Mirella and saluted with a pounded fist to her chest. "Sister!" she called, "We are mustering together our forces here. We've pulled back our patrols to await your orders," she explained. Svella was nowhere in sight, she realized, leaving her the one they were turning to.

"When the God-King returns, he will find this city to be truly his," she promised as she strode confidently towards the other women. She hadn't a lot of battle experience, but she knew the Aristeans. Their panic. Their fear.

They were falling, just like her former home had fallen, and they were making a last ditch effort to save themselves through self-destruction. "Any who refuses to swear to the God-King will be made example of."

The Raven Guard—those concubine-warriors and religious zealots—threw up their fists and cheered to her words. Their enthusiasm had not dimmed. Not in the least.

~~

The coming days put that to the test. The same young recruit who'd met her on her return from the cathedral that day met her again, breathless as always as she delivered her news at such a galloping pace. "Sister," she said saluting, "we can't pin the rebels down. They attack us from homes and alleyways without any pattern we can find. We can't catch them in an open battle. They hurl arrows, rocks and anything they can get at us but disappear before we can strike back decisively," she said, frustration obvious on her youthful features. Nimala, as Mirella had come to know her, looked to her for guidance.

She'd grown more comfortable in her role, more confident, and even at the advancing stages of her pregnancy, she'd been kept busy with stamping out what fires she could. She would do her God's work, and was grateful for the task.

She stood staring out the window and flicked the token the princess had given her between her fingers. "They have archaic magics, and who knows how they're communicating. I think we can lure them," Mirella paused her motions. "We need to send a message to the rebels, that there's a weak point. Freedom. A way to reclaim their Princess and their supplies. Find the old aqueduct, Nimala. See to it they find out about their path to glory. I trust you can see to the fact that they won't survive after that?" she asked.

The tall but relatively slender woman blinked, "In a battle the Raven Guard shall not fail, sister," she said without hesitation. "But... how will we get them to believe such a ruse?" Like most of her other sisters, Nimala did not grasp subtleties of warfare like subterfuge.

She pulled out the paper that the princess had given her, eyes scanning over the words, "Just plan the trap, sister. I'll have a letter within the hour that will convince them."

# CHAPTER 18

Things moved quickly from there. The city was lit up again by torches and fires as she made her way down to the old section of the city. None of the other Raven Guard could be used for such a mission. They were too obvious, their height and features marking them as towering northerners. And whom amongst the Aristean's could she trust for such a vital mission?

Donning the ratty old robes she wore to see the princess, that could do little to hide her pregnancy, she approached the crumbling old aqueduct structure. It looked unused, the stonework jutting out of the Aristean Mountains. It wasn't until she had wandered about there for some time looking for the entrance that she heard a voice, harsh and masculine. "What're you doin' wandering around out here?"

"The Princess sent me," she whispered, glancing

over her shoulder to make sure she wasn't being followed. She'd become such a natural actress in such a short period of time, though really, wasn't her whole life an act? Putting aside her own emotions and thoughts to please the noble lords and a spoiled princess?

"Please, let me pass. If they catch me," her voice hitched.

There was silence then until she heard in the shadows the sound of murmuring. They were cautious, and knew better than to whisper, for whispering carried further.

When finally they spoke however, it was with some hope to their scepticism. "Come over here," and she heard then a light creak coming from the stonework beneath the aqueduct, like the sound of a door.

Following after it she entered and once it closed the room lit up showing her a small stone entryway, buttressed by wood. There was a door that led further in, but this was obviously the start of the rebels' hideout. "Explain yourself," said the same man as before, pulling back his hood and revealing a stubbly but handsome face. Obviously a man of the Aristean working classes.

She wouldn't feel pity for them, and her hand stretched out to give him the letter, to show him the ring, "I'm the Princess's handmaiden. She's given me this to come to you, to tell you of a hidden way into the castle." Mirella stared at him, her eyes pleading.

The man looked at the offered letter and ring, his eyes went wide and it was obvious he understood the significance of such rich paper and a fabulous ring. "This is..."

Before he could finish though the other man stepped forward, the source of the other voice. This man was very different. It was obvious he was noble born, for who else could wear such rich clothes and spend so much time shaving and caring for his hair in a time of rebellion. "Let me see that," he demanded.

Mirella's heart raced as he opened the letter and studied it, scrutinized it. Moving to one of the candles he held the ring up to it, examining it with the eye of a jeweller as he checked.

After such a long wait he said. "It's real," then looked back to her. "So it's true then," stepping over to her. "The quake has opened a gap we can use to break into the palace armoury and cells. We could free the priest, princess and arm ourselves with real weapons to take back our city?" It was a question, but already she could detect the rising authority in his voice, as if he was ready to claim responsibility for this brilliant new plan then and there.

She simply nodded dumbly, back to playing the role of the simple serving woman. Being in this man's presence assuaged her guilt, her concern. He was one of *them*. "Please, you must save us."

The nobleman had no more to say, he saw her for what she appeared—a servant—and rushed off into the old structures beyond. She could hear his voice bellowing out, but it was the dark haired man that came to her. "Is it safe for you to go back? You can stay here with us until the palace is retaken," he offered.

Despite it all, despite her utter devotion to her God, her loathing of the nobles, and her distrust of everyone else, she'd only been able to cope with the horrors surrounding her by ignoring them. By pushing aside the fact that they couldn't get enough food through the mountains, by trusting that once he rightfully ruled the land he could begin to rebuild and care for the people. By understanding the reality of war, and poverty.

She couldn't stand to look at the man that looked at her with such kindness, and she felt her throat constrict.

She didn't want to kill these people. She didn't want to be responsible for their deaths, but she would do it. She believed in her God. She believed in Kulav. She knew there would be peace and prosperity that Ariste had never known before, welcoming in a new era of strength and devotion, rather than catering to the whims of the affluent.

And people would die because of it. Because of her.

"There's much I need to do," Mirella finally whispered, her vocal cords taut. "Thank you for your kindness."

The man nodded and guided her back to the door, "I understand. We all have much to give so that we might live like people again," he said. "Gods speed you, brave maid," he said, snuffing out the candle before opening the door and releasing her back into the night.

Tears fell, and she did nothing to stop them. She'd been so brave and confident, ever since he'd left, yet every time she met with an Aristean, she left with tears. She mourned for them, for their insolence and for their stubbornness, but by the time she reached the Concubine-Warrior's tent once more, her green eyes were hard once more.

~~

The attack came in the middle of the night as Mirella predicted. They came through a gap in the wall that the quake had indeed created, though since the Raven Guard had sealed it up immediately in their immense discipline, she had to have it ordered reopened just for the trap.

From the palace parapets she watched with her sisters as the rebels advanced through the gardens. When she gave the order a blood curdling cry went up through her fellow sisters, they rose with bows at the ready as she'd intended and the rebels froze or ran for cover with futility. All the exits were blocked, and shield-maidens stood at the hole they came through with spears pointed at them.

It was over.

"People of Ariste," she declared loudly, her voice carrying over the rebels. The working class. The poor. The downtrodden.

The nobles' pawns, just like she.

"Your city has been taken, and will continue to be that way. As I speak, the nobles are being wiped out. There is no hope for them, but there is hope for you! I know it doesn't matter to you who you serve. One hand is as good as another, and I promise you. Fight for us. Fight for your future, and you will be rewarded."

She paused for a brief moment, "Food is scarce. Times are hard, but we can work together to make Ariste better. The Northerners lack agriculture, but you thrive at it. Stop fighting us so that we may work together, to rid us of our noble lords and their cruelties. Ariste can be yours. Truly yours," Mirella finished, her stance, her voice, so utterly certain. She believed what she was saying.

There was silence for a while and she felt her sisters grow anxious. They were used to fighting and killing, not to negotiation. When things had gotten tense and she feared it was hopeless one of the Aristean rebels rose up and the recognized the voice from the aqueduct. "We surrender. Our families need food. That is why we're here. There is no point in dying for anything less," he stated, sounding glum but resilient yet.

She was so thankful for that one man, for that one voice, and she nodded. "I grew up hungry, without food. Sold from one family to another before I was finally brought here, and I remember it too well. You have suffered long, but I will help you become strong again," Mirella said, her voice dipping at the personal nature of her disclosure.

There were no cheers this time. Her sisters did not understand her leniency but obeyed it, for she was respected now, and the rebels below were too battered, too desperate and broken to cheer such words. All they could do was wait.

# CHAPTER 19

Svella returned to Mirella the next morning, "The job is done, sister." She sounded so proud, the woman already looking more like the battle-hardened warrior she was before conceiving the God-King's child. "The noble leaders were wiped out," she declared with a slam of her fist on the table. "Damn it feels good to be back in action!" Mirella knew just how much it had troubled her that the giant of a woman had missed so much of the fight already.

She laughed, and for the first time in many days, she truly felt it reverberate through her. "I'm sure there will be more before he returns. Has there been any news?" she asked, that hope creeping into her voice. "What of the Seer?"

She wanted to ask what was her price. What had she paid for this? She resisted, though.

At that query the mighty Svella lost her spirit. "No further news, though the violence seems to be dying down now," she explained. "And no, the Seer has not moved of her own accord since, I'm afraid." It troubled her, for the Seer was a unifying force for the Raven Guard.

~~

The rebellion was quelled and the city returned to some form of peace following Mirella's trap. However time dragged. She grew more and more swollen with her impending birth, and no news had arrived.

She'd spoken to the princess, told her the prince was reported dead though she had no actual word of what happened on the other side of the mountains. It confirmed it for her though, for the princess broke down into tears and sobbed about how she hadn't heard from him since the week the attack should've happened.

So Kulav had succeeded on the field of battle. Just as she knew in her heart and as the Seer had said.

It had been useless talking to the delicate princess after that. She was a wreck, and would, with any luck, be ready for the God-King's return.

It was as Mirella relaxed one day, the weight of her pregnancy exhausting her, that the excited Nimala burst in on her talking with Svella. "He's coming!" She cried. "The God-King is returning from the west reaches of the mountains!"

"What?" she gasped, trying to stand far faster than her body would allow, sending her off balance for a moment, "When will he be here?" she asked, and already she was moving as if she could see him. Her heart fluttered, and excitement buzzed under her flesh.

They emerged out into the cool morning air, Nimala talking excitedly, "The outriders reported seeing his banners just hours behind them!" She said, a great smile on her face. "He's coming back to us," she murmured in a dreamy voice, and Mirella realized then this sister hadn't had her opportunity to meet him before he went on his expedition.

Mirella smiled, as if her life had suddenly brightened. Become worth living once more, and she reached out to stroke Nimala's hand. "As we knew he would, sister." Her hand ran over her stomach, reassuring the child that stirred within.

# CHAPTER 20

When the God-King's forces returned at last, after being gone for months, the whole of the remaining guard were out in force in their full battle regalia. Horns sounded that echoed off the mountains and his banners fluttered from almost every building top. It was as glorious a return for the conqueror as she could muster, and she watched from the palace walls as his horse and following riders wound up through the city towards him.

When at last he led the way into the palace courtyard he looked as glorious as she remembered him. His armour seemed nicked and more worn, but he looked as stunning as ever. Those great raven plumes swaying in the air as he rode directly to her with confidence. She saw that grin on his face even before he slipped his helm free. He was back. Back for her.

Her movement was slower, her body nearly ready to burst with the heavy weight of his child, but that smile she gave him was nothing but radiant. Her love shone through, and that space she'd tucked aside, that deep loneliness was edged away.

As she moved through the palace walls, down and towards the courtyard, her heart swelled, and when at last her hands grazed him, her throat constricted. "Your Greatness," she breathed out.

The mighty warlord put an arm around her pregnant form and with great strength and care scooped her up against him, kissing her before all the assembled soldiers. It was a deep and passionate embrace, and she knew that her longing hadn't been one-sided. A well of intense desire was bubbling forth from him as that dark man kissed her deeply and stole her breath.

When at last he broke their embrace he gave her a grin, slipping his dark gaze down over her swollen belly with intense pleasure. "Go. Run me a bath," he commanded. "Bring a tray of fresh meats and a scrub brush, you shall tell me everything."

Even though he'd made her swoon, she found a great pleasure in doing his bidding. Her almond shaped eyes gazed at him for only a moment before her feet found the ground and she was moving back through the castle. Excitement carried her and made her feel lighter on her feet, despite her advanced pregnancy, and she could already feel that familiar heat between her legs.

He was home.

# CHAPTER 21

The tub which she set for him was formerly that of the royal family. It was heated from some vein of molten rock within the mountain itself, and the massive pool—for it was far too large to be a tub—was fit for a God. He reclined in the steamy water, his gorgeous physique, so brimming with hard muscle etched in perfect, detailed lines, standing out so prominently to her as she sat on the edge, scrubbing over his shoulder.

"You have done well," he said in a husky groan, enjoying her touch, his long dark hair draped down his back as he rested an arm up around her. "You took control of a chaotic situation and kept the city under control. I don't know if the Raven Guard could have managed that without you," he said with a light, placid smile.

"I couldn't allow you to come home to disarray, Your Greatness. Not after all the work you'd done," her nose nuzzled him, that lovely olive skin brushing against his ebon flesh. "You deserve a bit of peace and relaxation after the battle. The Princess is aware of the Prince's demise. I pray she is in a more malleable mood with the loss of her forces."

All she wore was the scandalous mix of silver chains and transparent fabric. He scooped her up, taking control of her with such ease as he pulled her into the steaming water with him. He let it soak her meagre things as she was pressed to his lap, feeling that godlike manhood against her as he kissed her hard. "You have served me well," he said, brushing her dark hair from her face and eying her with such desire and appreciation. "You were faithful when you could have turned against me and perhaps shifted the tide."

It hadn't even occurred to her, and her mouth found his throat, her body so eager against him. She was his, body, mind, and soul, and her arms wrapped around him, that pregnant orb pressing into his hard abs. "I mean every word I say to you, Your Greatness. You are the reason I exist. You are the tide, the spring rain. The one all should worship," her mouth ran along his jaw. "We will have crops this year, and it is because of your graciousness. I offered them a stay of execution, but you are the reason they will live. Our lives, our future. We entrust these things to you. It's only fair we mind them when you're gone."

It wasn't the way of the Ka'reem to offer mercy or forgiveness. They knew nothing of farming, only hunting and tending animals. But he did not question her decisions while he was away, only offered his quiet acceptance.

And his throbbing desire.

Squeezing her in his powerful arms, those hard muscles jabbing into her all around, he was careful of the life in her womb, suckling her lip as he probed her mouth with his tongue. A hand came to one of her large breasts, squeezing the full mound, so tender with its milk.

There was such need in him, and he lifted her, rising up onto his knees in the steamy pool, turning her away from him and placing her hands on the edge of the stonework so that she bent forward. Feeling his dark hands run up her arms and over her full form was such bliss, and he felt out every inch of her, as if rediscovering her at last.

She didn't quiet those moans, the sighs of pleasure and joy at his battle hardened hands, her body quivering against him. She wanted this, and had spent the long months of his absence craving him. Needing him.

Never had it occurred to her to bed with someone else, nor even to pleasure herself in the dark of night. It wouldn't be the same, and how wet she was, even as the water tried to lap it away, attested to her built up desire.

"Your Greatness," she whimpered. "I missed you."

One of his fingers hooked into her flimsy undergarment, pulling it aside to reveal her puffy, darkened folds. She felt one of his arms hook up in under her chest, his hand palming one of her large tits, squeezing as she felt that bulging thickness press to her.

So sweet were his dark, gravely words in her ear, "I thought of you often when need shook me," and she knew it was true. He was above false compliments; he didn't need such things with her.

Pushing into her she felt that massive cock, so far beyond any other man's, pry her folds open again. Though he had never been able to fit his full length inside her, even less fit now as her full womb pushed down, yet it didn't keep him from moaning with his own satisfaction at that tight cling.

She'd been so faithful to him, and yet she was surprised by how much it enhanced the experience. She almost felt like a virgin once more, untouched and innocent, even as she swelled with his child. Her moan was one beyond any other sweetness, beyond pain or simplistic, animalistic pleasure. It was love and devotion, bliss beyond understanding, and her hands gripped the edge of the bath.

"Every night, you were the first thing I dreamed of. Every morning, you were the first thing I saw. I knew you would make it home before your child was born," she said.

It was wrong in the eyes of her sisters to spill the God-King's seed fruitlessly in an already pregnant womb, but it didn't stop either of them from doing so and enjoying it. His hand grasped her teat, squeezing so delightfully, the other moving down over her generous hip and ass as he began to pump his godlike length into her.

He was so gentle for a man of his size and with his need, careful of the life within her, but still that throbbing dick beat into her with a fast increasing pace. His husky voice such a delight on her ear as it groaned each word out, "None of the young ones can hold a candle to your devoted lust. To your beautiful form," he bit her neck then, inhaling deeply through his nose as he stifled his moans on her flesh.

She whimpered with her need, and his words made her cunny tighten around him, those muscles massaging him so lovingly. She swallowed against his mouth, against the feel of that warm, heated breath over her olive flesh, and she knew she was in heaven.

She'd been waiting so long for just this, to be his once more, and it felt so right to have his body pressed against hers so tightly. Mirella fought back an overwhelming urge to cry his name, to tell him all she'd done, all she wanted to do just to have him back. Of the fear when the mountain collapsed, of that sense of failure and worry, but she didn't.

All she did was cry out his name, his true name, in a husky, lust ridden voice, following it up with "Your Greatness." The words—his name, his title— were one in the same. He was born of a woman, but that didn't lessen who he was. What he was.

He came in her then, clenching her tit and bucking his hips. Kulav, the God-King, spilled his seed within her fruitlessly, but so satisfyingly. His pleasure was thick on the air, and she knew she brought him such joy. More even than the pristine young virgins he took, her mature form, so ripe with his child, milked him of his essence and made him shake with satisfaction.

It didn't stop though, his long absence drove him on and he pumped his shaft into her without pause. She knew it wouldn't end then, or soon. He had to have her again. Again.

# CHAPTER 22

The God-King's return went fluidly. He never showed the slightest displeasure with her choices while gone, did not countermand a single one of them. He went about revitalizing his forces and getting the city into shape.

"From the north we'll bring in our remaining herds," he explained to the chieftains gathered around his command table, pointing to a map. "We need the extra meat and cheese to help feed the citizens as best we can."

Mirella was kept with him at nearly all times now. Nothing was kept from her, she'd proven her worth. Though as he spoke she felt it happen. Her water broke and pregnancy was upon her at last.

She thought back, for that brief, surprised second, and what she'd said to Svella those weeks ago.

Finally.

Her grin broadened and she felt no shame for being in such a delicate position near such powerful men. Instead she touched her God's arm, and as he turned to her, giving her his attention immediately, he seemed to understand everything with just the look on her face.

# CHAPTER 23

The pregnancy had been hard. If ever she doubted Svella's hard time—which of course she hadn't—that was put to rest when she birthed yet another son for her God and King.

Kulav had kept near her much of the time in the week following her birth, and she saw the light glimmer of pride in her and his new son as she cradled the boy. He kissed her head and looked to the child against her bosom, so dark. His skin, though so fresh and new, nearly matched that of his fathers. He was far more like Kulav than Svella's child had been, that woman's pale northern skin having diluted his tone.

Mirella had been lucky enough to have known bliss before, but that completion of her family, that natural process of creating something from both of them was different. She knew how pleased he was, and she'd always wanted a child. She had tried to push it aside as it grew less likely, but now that it was finally a reality, she let herself feel true joy.

"He looks like you," she murmured, that sleepy, happy daze making her eyes look lustier.

With a soft kiss to her forehead, the powerful Kulav stroked her hair tenderly. "You will name him Kulav'ar," he said firmly, for though it was tradition for the Ka'reem women to name their children, his mind was set. "It means Son of Kulav," he explained, and the significance of such a thing was not lost. How could it be? For though he had seeded many women—all of the Raven Guard and many more—none of the children had he claimed his own in any manner.

Her dark lashes descended over her eyes, and that wide smile, those hidden tears were sweet, tender affection. She nodded and swallowed in a breath. "Kulav'ar," she murmured, her finger clasped in the palm of her young infant. "Thank you."

# CHAPTER 24

One thing she could not ignore, even as she tended to her new child, was the growing sense of unease. Though the God-King was back, and with a mighty victory against the Empire, he knew it was not over yet.

"Your Greatness," bowed one of the chieftains, "our men have explored out the collapsed tunnels and found a way through. It is not enough for an army, or even a small raiding party, but it was enough to gather intelligence."

"Well," demanded the ebon deity, "what have they to report?"

The hairy barbarian leader shifted uneasily. "The Empire has amassed a new army on the other side of the mountains. They are working on excavating the blockage and..."

The God-King was tired of waiting, "Spit it out! Or be trampled beneath my horses hooves," he demanded darkly.

"And they are sending forces around the mountain."

"Which way?"

"Both," the chieftain replied.

He didn't need to ask how many. For the Empire did nothing in small measures. If the first invasion failed, then this next would be three times as large at least. With the powers of the witches and the genius of her master, even that would be insurmountable. There was only one out, and they all knew it.

Mirella cursed. That spoiled, pampered, stubborn brat. Mirella's strength was returning, her body slowly going back to her pre-pregnancy figure, but she'd not managed to find the will to deal with Princess Anabelle. Her eyes looked to Kulav imploringly, her tongue lancing her lips. "I will try again."

With a shake of his head he said, "No," firmly. "It is pointless." She knew it as well as him, but when there were no other options...

It was then it came to her, the Seer's voice. Though somehow she knew it wasn't the woman speaking to her now. It was a memory that had been implanted into her as she joined the other witches in their spell on that day months ago. It was the solution to their problems.

"I know what to do," she said.

# CHAPTER 25

Mirella left her sisters inside, hearing their chanting as she shut the door to the repaired chapel. The Seer was still unconscious, had not awoken since their last casting, but still she was like a focal point of their efforts even in her helpless state.

Mirella left them, shutting the door as she looked up to Kulav. The God-King gave her a steady look, "All our fates rest with you," he said with firm trust, and absolute faith.

"I won't disappoint you," she said, and she sounded as certain as he, that small smile teasing her lips. She moved to him, leaning up and pressing her mouth to his, her tongue probing him as though she were saying goodbye before she took a step back.

"Goodbye, my God," she murmured.

They'd made their farewells already; her flesh

still stung and ached from it. He didn't shed a tear, but she saw his stoic gaze flicker for just a moment. The most she'd ever seen his hard male eyes falter.

# CHAPTER 26

In the Princess's room Mirella found the young
woman in quiet contemplation. Still so young and
delicate, she looked to be over her recent troubles at
long last, though was slow to acknowledge her.
"What can I do? My prince is dead, the passage is
sealed... it's all over, Mirella. I can't do anything... not
a thing." By which she meant there was nobody to
take her orders.

"Princess," Mirella moved over to the woman
and began stroking her hair like she had in the days
before all this, bringing her brush to tenderly work
out the tangles. "I've not been honest with you," she
said softly. "I've been working on my own plan to
free you."

The fair young Anabelle looked to her slowly,
"What?" she said, as if lost in a dream, her light voice

barely carrying to her.

"There's a holdout of nobles... they lived through it all and they're awaiting you, but there's no way you can leave this castle, this room. If they find you," she frowned, shaking her head as she brushed out another blond curl. "I've found a way, though. It will sound strange, my darling Princess, but you trust me, don't you?"

The slender princess turned on her seat towards her, hope rising in her as those blue eyes widened. "You can get me out to them?" she said, and Mirella saw a tremble in the young woman's hands as excitement rose.

"Yes, and you can be off, safe and happy while they retake the city," she paused, licking her lips. "Princess, I've been gifted my freedom. I've had a child..." she trailed off as though it were too painful to think of before regaining her ability to speak, "I'm free to go. But you are so much more important. I've... I've found a way for you to go free in my stead. I will suffer for you, Princess."

The foolish girl blinked and looked her over, somehow having not realized that her former servant—whom she'd known almost all her life—was no longer pregnant. "They're letting you go," she repeated meekly. It was obviously a lot for the young woman to wrap her mind around, but she knew the tales of how women who survived their pregnancy were granted freedom. "How?" she asked, her voice building back to its usual command in that one, simple word.

From out of her pocket, Mirella took out of a

long, silver amulet, letting the chain drape between her fingers. "Princess, this necklace is enchanted. It will let us switch bodies, so that you may escape, free of scrutiny." Her breathing hitched as she looked at the young, fair princess, so different from herself. Those big, blue eyes. That long, golden hair. The ivory flesh.

She didn't covet those things. She was happy and comfortable in her own body, with the dark, olive flesh and her devious eyes, that long, glossy black hair. And those tiny marks that her pregnancy had still left her. She loved her body, yet this was something she was doing for greater reasons.

This was her sacrifice.

With hesitant fingers the curious princess touched the amulet. "What sorcery is this?" she murmured, not expecting an answer. She wet her pink lips then looked Mirella over.

She knew what the pale, royal waif was doing. She was debating with herself on whether she wished to downgrade herself to a servant's older form. "I don't know, Mirella..." she said hesitantly.

"Your freedom, Princess," she knelt down in front of the woman, her green eyes imploring the young Princess. "Please, it's killing me seeing you locked up here, away from your people. They're losing hope without you. They need you," tears threatened her vision as she begged.

A lifetime of serving this petulant girl had taught her how to manipulate her. "It's reversible, right?" she asked, lifting the amulet and studying it intently.

"Yes, Princess," she said in a calming tone. Both

needed to consent. To trust one another. To want the switch to occur. Mirella's words were absolutely honest, and her fingers grazed the noble's hand, "Your people need you."

Anabelle studied the pendant long, lost in her own indecisiveness. It was too long really, considering how obvious the choice seemed, but at last she nodded, her beautiful young face contorted into firmness. "I'll do it. My people need me," she said to Mirella, her azure gaze crystalline and hard.

Mirella resisted the urge to roll her eyes, and took the chain from the woman, slowly descending it over Anabelle's head, "For the good of Ariste, I do this."

The princess arched her spine and stood prim and proper, the fullness of her royal form returned. "The people shall remember this. It will be told in tales long after my rule has ended," she said with absolute certainty.

Her harder hands took the pampered flesh of Anabelle, her fingers so light as she grazed the flesh, her voice becoming low as she began chanting. Her voice met with the others of the circle below, the stone of the palace not able to keep the sisters of the Raven Guard from joining their powers together.

All about them the air seemed to thrum, the air vibrating as if it were countless little pebbles that shook with some mighty energy.

"What's happening?" she heard the voice of the princess so faint, as if distant and far off.

# CHAPTER 27

The entire city showed up that day for the wedding. The imperial army sent forth its own representatives, minor nobles considered expendable enough for the task.

Ariste rung with the bells of the cathedral as the smiling couple emerged onto the steps of the great holy building. The new Queen and wife looking even more dainty and pale than usual in contrast to the great, dark visage of the God-King, her husband.

Anabelle was slender, and that long, white dress felt like it flowed down over her form unhindered by womanly curves, the breeze catching it and making it dance against her body. Her hand held tight to her husband's as her pretty, pink lips twisted into a smile, tears of joy making her blue eyes twinkle even more vibrantly.

Flowers were twisted through her golden hair. Little pink and purple blossoms stuck out around her braids and curls, the updo so elaborate and painstakingly done. The soft anklet of raven feathers went unseen as it caressed her bare feet, making her seem even shorter compared to him. Her God. Her King. Her Husband. Her Kulav.

A lifetime of serving royalty had prepared for that day, and none doubted her as she strode through the nobles, or rode up the hill to her palace. She knew all the things to say, and though the body was foreign to her, she knew how to wield it primly.

# CHAPTER 28

That night she met him in the royal bedroom. Forms had to be followed. The Empire's representatives would insist on everything being done perfectly. Even the virginal shroud had to be provided for them, as any pretence of illegitimacy would be used to swoop in and claim the city.

The God-King studied her in the light of that magnificent room, held her dainty hand as his eyes roamed over her. "So frail," he said in a firm but low voice, still reeling with the changes in her.

He looked resplendent in his shimmering outfit. It was, in essence, a more ostentatious version of his battle wear. The glimmering raven's feathers so sleek, gilded in silver. They would be crowned on the morrow assuming the Empire found no objection. Officially the King and Queen.

"It's strange," she agreed, but her hands moved along his chest so readily, so eagerly, and he could tell it was her. None would have the brazen audacity to meet his eyes like she did; none would have the authority to let her palms press against his flesh. "Kulav'ar will look so different from me, now," she lamented, but her mouth sought out his, her tongue glancing against him.

The Princess' body was hers, now. And she gave it freely to him.

Scooping the delicate young form of his wife into his arm, he pressed her to the bare flesh of his ashen skin, letting her pale form feel him out as he carried her to the massive bed. It was a king's bed, and could've fit two dozen waifs like her now, but it was all theirs.

He laid her out, slid his hard hands up her slender calves and milky white thighs, pushing her stunning dress up as he eyed her. Through it she heard the material of his pants stretch with his growing arousal, the leather straining. "There shall be more children," he said, though with the tone he knew it was little compensation for her.

The youth did provide her many more opportunities. The Princess was still so vibrant and nubile, and she knew her form would contort so attractively. Those blue eyes of hers stared up at him as her legs parted, revealing the smooth, blonde pelt between her legs. Her body was ready for him, and she bit her lip to suppress a grin.

"I never thought I'd have to go through this again," she admitted shyly.

A grin spread across his face at that remark, and as she watched him roll his shoulders back and undo the clasps of his belt, pulling open his pants, she saw that massive, dark girth fall out so heavily. "This time," he said, lowering himself down over her so that its bulging crown, so slick and dark grazed her pale blonde tuft of pubic hair, "it shall be a lot worse."

She saw his teeth then as he nudged himself against her thin hymen. Such a tiny, puffy little slit seemed so vulnerable compared to him as he prepared to rip it asunder.

She'd given birth, she knew of pain, but something about the prospect of him taking her virginity thrilled her, even at the promised pain. She thought back to the women she'd helped him deflower, to those concubines she'd wetted for him, and grew heated against his thick crown.

"My husband," she murmured, "Don't take me gently."

He didn't.

That bulbous girth tore into her, forcing her narrow, virginal canal to widen in his wake. He gave such a low, husky groan of delight at it, the pain and pleasure so sweet. Then, pausing in their marital bliss, they looked to the obscene sight of his bulbous dark cock protruding out of her puffy pink slit.

No longer did she sport those wide child bearing hips. Now it was such a slender frame, and it made his penetration of her look all the more lewd. He began to buck his hips and pump his shaft into her, groaning with satisfaction as his pace grew so fast.

She screamed, partly because she knew the

Princess would scream. Only they could hear that arousal that ran with it, that secret, shared bliss as she felt that thick cock piston into her. She couldn't lift her legs, couldn't hook them around him, but it was so sweet, and violent. The slender curves, the pale flesh of her body was in such contrast to him. In such contrast to her own body.

Kulav held little back, and the sound of his heavy balls slapping against her pert little ass resounded in the chambers, his husky breathing and moaning such a ruckus. They both know the Empire's representatives listened from the chamber outside the door. Everything was so official. But none of that stopped them from enjoying it, and he ripped her dress in his hard yank, trying to get at one of her petite breasts, mauling it with his hunger.

The dusty pink nipple was so hard against that small bit of flesh, her breasts not even a handful for the large man, though they were firm and supple. Her eyes fluttered closed as her warbling cry resounded around the chamber and tiny 'ows' peppered the air. He was hurting her, but the silent way she coaxed him on, the eagerness of that hot, wet entrance were so sweet as the blood dripped from her and soiled the sheets below.

Just as it should.

It was such a roar when he came, as if he too were putting on some show for their observers. The beast in Kulav let loose as he shook with his climax, loosing such a torrent of thick, virile cum into her fertile young cunny.

It was a strange experience for Mirella—now

Anabelle—and not just because of the switch of her body. It was as if she could feel herself on some level beyond what a person should. She could sense his seed working into her with such tenacity, and had this sense that if she willed it, she could deny it a hold within her. Instead she let it runs its course, and that night she knew, by some power, that she had conceived.

# CHAPTER 29

The coronation was even bigger than the wedding. The Empire had acquiesced to the new rulership, for there were no grounds to deny it. The princess was now the saviour of her people, sparing them another arduous battle, negotiating for food relief from the imperial forces, and, to top it off, she offered them all a traitor.

None objected to the offering of the middle aged servant. The Raven Guard, her sisterhood, were the only ones other than Kulav and her who knew the truth of who she was, and so they accepted it. But to appease the Empire and show the good faith of the new rulers, "Mirella" would serve the rest of her days raving in some dark dungeon that she was the true princess.

Such things were bittersweet, however. She

thought she'd paid her price, but she was wrong. Her own son no longer recognized her as mother, and though so young he looked at her with such an odd gaze.

The new life swelling within her delicate body, elevation to the status of a queen and the love of her God-King would have to suffice. In the late nights, though, when her husband slumbered beside her, she wondered at Kulav'ar, and what would come of the true son of Kulav.

# NOTE FROM THE AUTHORS

Thank you so much for reading and purchasing our story. We hope it made you squirm, and that once you recover, you'll take a look for more of our works available on http://www.jmkeep.com.

Did you enjoy yourself? Take a quick second to leave your opinion on Amazon and Goodreads!

**Connect with us:**

Website: http://www.jmkeep.com

Twitter: http://www.twitter.com/jmkeep

Facebook: http://www.facebook.com/jmkeep

Get three sexy, erotic shorts for for FREE by joining our Newsletter!

Lilah and Glaurakos don't trust one another. They have no reason to. With her angelic wings and his demonic horns they're undoubtedly enemies, though they have some part of their nature in common.

They're drawn to one another despite the odds

and the fact that they stumbled into a place that no mortal or god should tread. There's something wrong about the portal they entered and finding they can't leave without some magical implements, their bond has to forge deeper to make it out.

Will the turmoil of the strange world bring them together or rip them apart? The dangers of this new world are perilous yet their emotions and lust are far more frightening.

Warning: This fantasy novel contains steamy sex, devious demons, and atypical angels. It's a twisted romance at its core, and was inspired by Dungeons and Dragons/Forgotten Realms lore.

**On Fel Wings She Soars will be available in serial format beginning July, 2013! The full novel will be released in September, 2013**

# MORE BY J.E. & M. KEEP

**Standalone Shorts:**

After Office Hours – Blackmail
Pussy Cat Club – Rough Sex
A Night of the Arts – Exhibitionism/Pussy Worship
Hot Desert Daze – Gay M/M Submission
Don't Lie to Me – Infidelity/Cuckolding Fantasy
Wedding Present – Contemporary Interracial
Infidelity
The Lost Lagoon Prelude– M/F Twincest Romance
Blessing of Fertility – Divine Monster Breeding
Gangbang
Cock Worshipping Goddess – Demon Cock worship

**Series Shorts:**

*Anjasa Between Dungeons*
Cutting a Deal – Fantasy ménage erotica
Demon's Den –Demon/elf rough sex
Dragon's Lair – Dragon/elf cock worship

*Amy's Innocence*
Part 1 (Purity) – Deflowering
Part 2 (First Love)– Coming of Age
Part 3(Family) – Settling Down

*A Naughty School Girl Collection*
Tiffany's Detention - School girl / barely legal
Tiffany – Teacher's Pet – May December Domination
Tiffany's Daddy – Reluctant Daddy/Daughter Incest
Breeding Tiffany – Daddy/Daughter Breeding
Tiffany's Blackmail – Forced Sleep Sex
Tiffany's Brother – Brother/Sister Taboo
Tiffany's First Gangbang – Barely Legal Gangbang

*A Dark Fairy Tale*
Bad Wolf, Be Good – Twisted Romance

**Erotic Novellas:**

Outcast – Dark Fantasy / Taboo
A Son's Devotion – Mother/Son Incest
Brought the Stars to You – Sci-fi Romance
Bound as the World Burns – Post apocalyptic BDSM
Erotic Romance

**Erotic Novels:**
Vile Wasteland – Post Apocalyptic Erotic Romance
Wheel and Deal – Dark Fantasy

**Coming Soon:**
Series Shorts: Enslaved– Mind Control
Novel: On Fel Wings She Soars
Novella: The Lost Lagoon
Novel: False Shades

# BIOGRAPHY

J.E. and M. Keep write dirty, filthy, smutty erotica. With a passion for all things sci fi/fantasy, and a desire to see what characters do when others fade to black, they set out to explore the most sexual, titillating and sometimes terrifying encounters. The plots are contemporary, fantasy, or science fiction, but they all have one thing in common: they're hot.

From dark and taboo smut to coming-of-age's lust, from twisted love stories to tragic tales of self destructive needs, they explore the fact that not all 'Ever Afters' are happy, and not everyone's idea of happy is the same.

Come explore the limits of erotica and discover new desires from the smutty minds of J.E. & M. Keep. They can be found on their website at http://www.darkfantasyerotica.com/.

9 781988 619118